The Lownsbury Chronicles

The

Machine

Second Options

It had been harrowing ordeal.

Somehow, Larimer Lownsbury had miraculously escaped the deadly clutches of Senator Schulte's sadistic daughter; Samantha.

Abandoned to imprisonment for witchcraft in 17th century Salem, Samantha now faced a future of pain and torment in the dank, dark cells of a New England dungeon. Her only hope; that her father can find her before she devolves into a ghoulish creature. And her only solace is a vow of revenge.

A debt to be repaid in blood!

From the moment Larimer Lownsbury, Will Masters and Jack Sterling said their goodbyes and flashed into time inside of a little café in downtown Brooklyn, their one mission was to keep Schulte from finding his daughter.

But that seemingly simple task was far more daunting than our heroes could have ever imagined and now each of them are in different times, facing their own, dark demons. And their seemingly simple mission is unraveling before their eyes.

In the continuing saga of the *Lownsbury Chronicles*, we take a step backwards and discover what led our heroes to the mysterious Orb and how Senator Schulte managed to rescue his sadistic daughter from a crippling demise.

Along the banks of the Nile in Ancient Egypt, one of the greatest stories ever told is unfolding.

Lurking through the deadly streets of London's Whitechapel, an unspeakable terror is being unleashed.

In *Second Options*, more secrets are revealed, more questions are answered and more truths are given.

From Baghdad to Brooklyn and beyond, Larimer Lownsbury, Jack Sterling and Will Masters travel through time in an ongoing effort to confront mankind's darkest adversary:

Himself!

The Lownsbury Chronicles

The

Machine

Second Options

W.C. WALLBAUM

The Machine; Second Options

W.C. Wallbaum

First Edition Copyright: 2020 by W.C. Wallbaum

Revised Edition: 2023 by W.C. Wallbaum

Cover art and illustrations by: Cat's Imaging and Design

The Bowtie Principle and The Syndromes of Civilization and related graphics are the exclusive creation and copyright of

Wall To Wall Publishing

Walltowallpublishing.com

ISBN's

EBook: 978-1-7331256-2-8

Paperback: 978-1-7331256-3-5

The Lownsbury Chronicles:

By W.C. Wallbaum

The Machine; First Strike

The Machine; Second Options

The Machine; Third Rule

Lownsbury's Lecture; A Compendium
Featuring:
The Bowtie Principle
And
The Syndromes of Civilization

Acknowledgements:

Special thanks go to all of my family:

My wife, my mother and my daughters have all had unique perspectives and offered invaluable assistance in the creation of this manuscript and its editing.

My sons: whose artistic drive never fails to inspire me - and their respective working, singular knowledge that helped create significant portions of this work.

And to my dad who made a fascination with history - and the fiction that could be crafted within its framework - come alive in me since I was a child.

Among the many resources in which I have engaged to create my version of historical events, special acknowledgement goes to the late Immanuel Velikovsky and his study and theory's of the ancient world.

And of course the historians and scribes of antiquity; their souls live on in their writings - if we will only take the time to appreciate them.

A well deserved appreciation also goes to Pixabay.Com.

"A Violet From Mother's Grave" - Written and composed by Will H. Fox, c.1881. The last song known to have been sung by Mary Kelly

DIRECTORY:

The cities and peoples of ancient Egypt, and how they are known today:

Kemet = Egypt

Kusi = Kush

Black River = Nile River

Waset = Thebes

Mennefer = Memphis / Cairo

Wilderness of Sin = Sinai

Retjenu = Levant

Qis = Cusae

Djahy = Southern Levant

Great Green = Mediterranean Sea

Iunu = Heliopolis

Naharin = Mitanni

Urasilm = Jerusalem

Kubna = Byblos

Shedat = Faiyum Oasis

Fenkhu = Phoenicia

Sea of the Dead = The Dead Sea

Jebel Musa = Mount Sinai

Given Life = Still Living

Justified = Deceased

"Science is not only compatible with spirituality; it is a profound source of spirituality."

-Carl Sagan

Authors Note

The history of Egypt is the history of mankind. Like most great empires, its past was replete with periods of peace and incredible artistic mastery; innovations and marvels. And times of war over resources, territory and encroachments. It had periods of invasion - both soft and barbaric. It birthed philosophers of great wisdom and ingenuity; Mathematicians of history's highest caliber, and warriors and peacemakers that were hailed as gods on earth. (Or what we came to refer to in our time period as *Saints*.) Their civilization literally spawned the Judeo-Christian religions that have endured throughout the Common Era.

They enjoyed their pets; they worked for the best for their children; their cities featured the finest of the world's greatest libraries and their universities offered the world the finest in education.

Its land was split in two - between Upper and Lower Egypt - and was reunited a number of times during their long existence. The Egyptian empire's orientation coincided with the flow of the Nile River. Its pathway originating in Ethiopia and winding north towards the Mediterranean Sea. Lower Egypt was thus situated north - around the river's delta - while Upper Egypt existed south of the great pyramids of Giza.

As the author has taken artistic liberty with the description of certain Egyptian traditions and people, a significant portion of this narrative nonetheless surrounds known historical events of antiquity.

A number of references are made to cities, peoples, and various areas in and around Egypt. With certain exceptions, the original Egyptian names and terminology were used throughout much of the following text. It is believed that the Ancient Egyptians referred to their land as **Kemet** (the Black Land ... due to the color of the fertile earth after the annual Nile Flooding) and themselves as **Remecht en Kemet** (People of the Black Land)

For the ease of reading, the author retained the use of the conventional name of Egypt - among other examples.

THE

MACHINE

Second Options

Part I

W.C. Wallbaum

Prologue

The Manuscript:

The room in which we sat was like none I had ever seen; masterpieces, from the deep past to the contemporary, filled the room. The man that sat across from me seemed to shimmer amongst the grandeur of the room, as if he were a part of it. I was spellbound before he even began to speak.

"I was known as Ta-Huti, although I was not born with that name," he said, solemnly. His eyes casting his face in a weary pallor.

He stared into a long forgotten time as he spoke, "Ta-Huti was actually a name given to me by a gracious queen of a long dead empire. And, while it is true that I have lived for centuries, since nearly the dawn of mankind in fact, I am not the only one."

I shifted nervously in my seat as he spoke. My phone propped in the space between us, recording every word. As I listened to the narrative that unfolded, I remember initially thinking that this was all far too incredible to believe. No one ever spoke like this with the intention of being believed. Unless - of course - they were certifiably insane.

But the more the man spoke, and the more time I spent in that incredible library, the more I came to understand that this was far more than an elegant fairy-tale. Everything about this man and the surroundings in which I found myself, dictated a need for belief; *of faith*. It had not taken long for my initial skepticism to have turned to one of astonishment.

"By now though, many of my fellow Elders have long gone," he continued with a heavy breath. "And I am one of the remaining few of my kind. I suppose one day I shall tire of this existence, or perhaps fall to some unknown or unnatural fate as many of my brethren have. But for now, I linger. Committed to help mankind as best as I am able. To help them see through their mistakes and as always, do my best in making sure a balance is maintained between the two brothers."

He sighed and went silent for a long moment. "When you have done everything else, what other goal remains?"

He reached over to a short coffee table that occupied the space in front of our chairs and where a pot of tea had been steeping. He poured

3

two cups, offering me one. I had not noticed before, but the cup and its matching set was of exquisite caliber. Delicate but quite durable; perfectly shaped and balanced. They were highly consistent with the rest of the furnishings and decorations of the ostentatious room in which we sat. There was no doubt that the entire tea set was hundreds of years old and absolutely priceless.

The man settled back in his chair, blowing across his cup before a delicate sip.

"This is actually the story of a manuscript," he continued. "A manuscript that I began writing so long ago." He then fell to silence, taking a long swallow of his tea. I couldn't tell if he had suddenly become lost in a memory, or needed a moment to pick carefully his next words. By now I was becoming used to his lingering pauses.

Finally - he resumed, "It is a document of history. Of events to which I was witness. Within its pages contain perhaps one of the greatest stories ever told. A story of the most pivotal moment in time that changed the world. It is the story of my beginning; of everyone's beginning, really."

He looked at me, his eyes like a portal into time. Ageless. Commanding. He seemed to shimmer again and a large, leather bound book magically appeared in his hands. He spoke the next words quietly, yet his voice brimmed with intensity, "The vast majority of mankind will never know where it started, young man. They will speculate and they will theorize." He patted the cover of the large bundle on his lap.

"But it all started right here."

One

∞

Mennefer, Kemet (Egypt); The Pyramid of Ra;
Date: Unknown

Cithimay stood quietly in the lingering twilight, staring up at the massive stone structure.
Remembering.

She had been here many times throughout her life, and each time the waste and decay of the once beautiful city seemed worse than the last.

The Black River - barely visible in the distance - so much further away now than she remembered - its path altered through the years. The lush gardens and forests that once spread as far as the eye could see, now gone. Covered beneath the sand's relentless encroachment. The desert's merciless onslaught threatening to bury even more of the crumbling buildings that held so many memories for her. Even the mightiest of stones that were once destined to stand the test of time were now lost to mother nature's persistent invasion.

But worse still were the people. Long gone were the descendants of Alysia that once occupied this land. Lost and buried to time. Nearly forgotten. But she remembered.

Her land had now been replaced with crowds of ignorant, unwashed bodies. Pressing together amidst their own filth and waste. Like animals waiting to be slaughtered.

It was disgusting.

But this visit was the first in such a long time to be filled with promise. The promise of a new life.

The promise of life.

The pyramid towered high into the sky in front of her. She could scarcely see the pinnacle from where she stood. She remembered how the walls had once glittered in the sunlight. Its golden, limestone laced facade, a breathtakingly blinding experience. But the conductive gold of the outer walls was gone now. The entire plateau showing the ravages of time and the relentless encroachment of the desert sand.

But she remembered.

The other massive pyramid that stood nearby had been built by Alysia but at a much later date than the first. It had been an effort to capture - and focus - the energy of the *Eye of Ra* to receiving stations around the globe. A naive effort to offer the world the energy and advancements that Alysia enjoyed. But much to the surprise of the citizens of Alysia, it proved to be an effort that was unappreciated and unwelcome.

Yes, she remembered.

Just a short distance towards the east and downhill from where she stood, were one of the stone remains of the two massive lions that once guarded the eastern gate to the city of Alysia. The deluge following the fall of her grandfather and his city - so long ago - had wiped one of the great beasts from the earth altogether and had long taken its toll on the remaining stone monument. Egyptian kings had later marred the orphan's once pristine carvings. Permanently scarring its original beauty.

She remembered as a young girl, marveling at the eminence of the golden beasts. The gleaming surfaces - hot and blinding in the midday sun - offered a welcome warmth that calmed her own savage soul. The bestial effigies that once whispered their calming susurrations of strength and endurance to her as they stood relentless guard to the incredible city that once occupied this hallowed ground, now weathered and wasted and all but forgotten.

But she remembered.

She remembered the stories of Alysia too. Of her grandfather - Ah-Tum. Of his retrieval and command of the *Great Eye of Ra*. How he placed the Eye into the pyramid, moving the giant stones into place with a power unfathomable - even to the eldest of Elders - encasing the Eye far at the top.

She remembered the stories of how Ah-Tum had taken his wife Evalana and together, had created the splendid city and empire of Alysia. How it and its people had flourished for untold generations. She remembered how her father - Ka-Yin - had demanded that the city be open to his own followers, but the council of Elders had refused. Insisting that only worthy and refined people could be part of Alysia's population.

She also remembered the pain she felt. Pain at how her father had been banished by the council for having desecrated the covenant with the Cratalis. For daring to sire her and her brother with a palace commoner. She would never forget the humiliation she felt - that she always felt - within the city of Alysia.

She remembered how her father had finally confronted Ah-Tum and - with the *Bracelet of Ra* - breeched the city walls - leading the primitive masses to conquer the once great empire.

But more than anything, she remembered the stories of the Cratalis and the power it held to render a person immortal. With the Cratalis, she could be unshackled from her father. She would be able to do as she pleased, travel at will and possess a power more than any would ever know.

The Cratalis had been all that she had ever desired. She had waited so long for this opportunity and soon, it would be hers. Soon, that foolish professor would retrieve the Cratalis from its hiding place. He would be vulnerable. It had all been part of her father's plan. A plan that had stretched across time. A plan that was eons old. A plan he had orchestrated as brilliantly as a finely tuned symphony.

She breathed deep the hot, desert air and smiled.

Soon she would have the precious elixir of life and her lifetimes of dreams would finally come true.

Soon.

Two

United States; Present Day

Some would have thought Bobby Hatfield a lucky man.

A lucky man, indeed:

Bobby Hatfield lived in the suburbs of Memphis with a beautiful wife and a baby on the way. He had a long standing job as a first-class welder in a long established firm. He had a nice house, nice cars, and quite a number of nice toys, including his prized possession - a classic, 1964 Chevy Impala SS with the original Turbo Fire 327 engine - that he had completely restored.

Yes, many considered him quite lucky.

But given the opportunity, Bobby Hatfield would tend to argue this point of view. In fact, in fits of candid confession and with the right drinking partner - *meaning anyone who would listen* - he didn't seem to share that seemingly objective opinion at all.

Yes, he made a good salary. And yes, he had a nice house. But it was too large a house than he could actually afford and every month was a challenge to make the payments. And as much as he loved his toys; the cars, the motorcycles, *et al*. He knew that his and his wife's spending kept them living paycheck to paycheck. Spending - to them - was an addiction that seemed impossible to overcome.

Now they were in their forties and Bobby had no savings, no retirement and no further hope of advancement and he was now too old for another company to even consider him.

Lucky indeed.

He hadn't asked for anything from anybody. Never. And he was proud of that fact. "*Too proud,*" his wife often said. So he was not only surprised but a bit annoyed at the interference into his life when he discovered that he had inherited a piece of property. And a historic property at that.

In Massachusetts, of all places.

'*What the hell was in Wayland, Massachusetts?*'

A great uncle of sorts apparently had no one to leave his estate to - except for Bobby. And now Bobby not only had his own affairs to attend to, he had to make time for the unfinished affairs of an uncle he never really knew.

Lucky?

Bobby had been contacted by a law firm in Boston nearly a month previous. The lawyer had been highly insistent that Bobby come to Wayland and make the needed arrangements for the disposition of the estate that his uncle had left him. Like it or not, Bobby was suddenly the proud - if not reluctant - owner of a piece of property in New England.

He had not expected much with the property but as he researched the home and the land it was on, he became hopeful that the property could help relieve some of their debt and pull him and his wife out from under the mountain of credit cards that seemed to be swelling on its own accord. And hopefully put a little extra coin in their jeans.

Hopefully.

Located thirty minutes west of Boston, the home was Semi-Rural - as North East homes tend to be in the suburbs of larger cities. It bordered several lots of tree lined roads and shared a subdivision of higher end homes. With every click of the mouse in researching the home, Bobby became increasingly hopeful that the sale of the property would bring relief to him and his wife and give them some much needed breathing room. Especially with a baby on the way. It seemed to be a beautiful neighborhood after all. And in a highly coveted part of town.

But when the pictures of the home arrived by courier from the trustee's office in Boston, his heart fell:

The home was in a state of severe disrepair; shabby and in need of paint - extremely overgrown and dilapidated. Water damage around most of the roof and eaves of the home was extensive. The lot was overgrown with trees and scrub bushes in an obvious attempt to conceal a *POS* that needed a lot of attention to put it back into livable condition. Even the land was in need of landscaping. In one of the pictures, Bobby could make out the remains of an old barn that appeared to be on the verge of falling down on its own.

And that was what he could see with marketing pictures!

'*Lucky my ass*!' He thought.

Bobby didn't want this burden. A messed up old house somewhere in Massachusetts?

Son of a bitch!

Born and raised in Memphis Tennessee, he preferred the south. It was too cold in New England and it was far too expensive a prospect to live in anyway. "*Too many goddamn liberals that couldn't seem to mind their own business*," as his father would say.

Jesus - and the taxes.

Inherited or not, even if he could afford to fix the house up he couldn't afford the taxes the state and county imposed. Much less the association dues. He had already received several letters demanding he do something about the shabby condition of the home and the ramshackle barn in his back lot, or the neighborhood association of the area would levy a heavy lien and do it themselves.

He already hated Massachusetts and he hadn't even left Tennessee. By the time he was done paying lawyers, at least two existing mortgages, property taxes and probate costs, not to mention a number of association liens, it would barely make the trip to Massachusetts worth it. In fact, it would probably leave them further in debt than they were before.

His uncle had certainly left him a white elephant.

"*Lucky my ass*," he repeated under his breath.

Maybe he could bring the property value up if he worked on the place, but he didn't have the time. His job at the welding shop wouldn't hold his position for that long and his wife did not want to move to Massachusetts any more than he did. He simply couldn't afford to stay in Wayland, but he also couldn't afford not to.

So in a compromise with his expectant wife, he had budgeted a week.

One week to tear down the old barn out back, throw a coat of paint on the house, fix a few things that would hopefully pacify the association and be on the earliest bus back to Memphis with some kind of check for his troubles.

And troubles indeed. The whole affair seemed like a whole lot of trouble from an uncle he barely knew.

Lucky Bobby Hatfield.

Staring at the barn at the rear of his new tree lined yard in Wayland, caused a heavy groan to escape Bobby Hatfield's barrel chest. God, what a mess - it was worse than he had imagined. Buried in a tangle of underbrush and what he was sure was a thunderous field of poison ivy, lay the remains of an ancient building. Its only remaining support was the trunk of an oak tree that had chosen that spot - probably 75 years ago - to sprout.

Stretching his neck to the point of cracking and donning a fresh pair of work gloves, Bobby spent a solid hour just breaking through the first layer of weeds and tangle of undergrowth. He eventually stumbled upon the dilapidated remains of a door - busted and tilted on ancient hinges. The thought that the building was an old outhouse crossed his mind and he knew he would come certifiably undone at the seams if he fell into an old *shit-pit*.

Pulling back a timber, Bobby began to saw through the first of many a rotten board in an attempt to gain access to the structure. By noon he was bathed in sweat and attracting the attention of an unmerciful swarm of mosquitoes, hornets and other insect life that infested the remains of the old building.

Lucky man here!

Once he had broken through to the inside, he realized that the ramshackle barn had probably been a caretaker's quarters. Old tools and iron bric-a-brac adorned the walls. A cheap broken plate here and a tin cup there - littered the floor.

And the smell!

"*Good Christ*!" He said aloud in disgust - holding his shirt over his nose.

There had been a variety of animal life that had become trapped inside the decrepit building and had finally succumbed to their fate. Their remains littered the floor.

Bobby continued to survey the interior - breathing through his mouth into his sweat soaked tee shirt - looking for anything of value that may have been left behind. Weather-beaten furniture along with skunk, rabbit, cat and raccoon carcasses seemed to be the only visible items.

But when he broke through an old cupboard - of what was once part of a kitchen - Bobby's eyes came to rest on something he had not expected to see.

'*Yes indeed, perhaps this trip wasn't a waste of time after all,*' Bobby thought to himself. Perhaps the little gem he had just uncovered - hidden for an untold number of years in the weathered tomb of decay and debris he now owned - held the answer to his dreams after all.

He smiled as he manhandled the heavy antique from its age encrusted hiding place. It looked like a treasure chest. *'And after all,'* - he thought - *'treasure chests always contained treasure.'*

Yes sir, perhaps this old box may just contain all the luck he needed. *A lucky man, indeed.*

Three

Baghdad, Iraq; 2002

Tentacles of darkness rapidly swallowed the last vestiges of sunlight that filtered across the desert plain as night engulfed the city streets of Baghdad. The heat of the day began to yield to a chill wind blowing in from the north. Several of the Iraqi Republican Guards trudged slowly from one end of the wall - high atop the Republican Palace - to the other. Their attention on high alert as they scanned the palace grounds. Each one tense in anticipation of the following evening - certain to be hectic with the visitation of the dignitaries that were due to arrive.

Between the moonlight and the palace searchlights, the Tigris River glittered as it flowed peacefully a mere hundred yards away. Captain Rashid Al-Sameer scanned the moving water from high upon the guard tower. He sighed. Another long night looking at the same skyline he had been living beneath for the last thirty years.

Rashid loved his country, to be sure. Its long history stretched beyond biblical times - with a rich legacy of which most Iraqi's were proud. It was the birthplace of modern man and the presumed cradle of civilization. A shining oasis in a vast desert of chaos, war - *and death*.

But Rashid was also quite fearful of the times that lay ahead. His leader had been growing more radical with each passing day. It was as if Saddam enjoyed poking the Americans in the eye every chance he got - somehow forgetting that it was by their will that he was still in power.

His saber rattling had grown to epic proportions, especially since his humiliating defeat in Kuwait. And now Saddam seemed intent on making bedfellows with forces that would ultimately turn the eyes of the United States once again, to Iraq. It was not a position Rashid wished for his beloved country.

A very high level meeting was scheduled to take place at the palace the following evening and Rashid had been told to expect some action from the Americans. But Captain Rashid was doubtful. Political propaganda had divided most Americans when it came to the disposition of Iraq. Their politicians appeared wishy-washy at best. And Rashid highly doubted that the American President would have the fortitude to make any kind of disturbance.

He pulled the binoculars from his face and lit a cigarette. His mind flashed to the Kuwait war and how the Americans had defeated them so handily. A humiliating encounter whose purpose only served to showcase the latest weaponry from the greatest force on earth.

But in the end, it had mattered little. America was a living contradiction of itself. A country of spoiled children who didn't have the good sense to use what Allah had allowed them.

Perhaps he shouldn't underestimate them, he considered. For as gentle and giving as the Americans were, they were true killers when their passions were aroused and Nine-Eleven had done just that. He could scarcely believe someone had been so foolish as to ignite that passion. And even more so, how Saddam could be so foolish as to invite those same fools here.

Rashid shook his head in silence. Perhaps he worried for nothing. The United States could not seem to keep their political house under control. Rashid highly doubted any reaction from them. He instinctively knew that one day America would no longer be the threat it was today. It didn't need any help from Saddam or any of his new found friends. It would eventually go the path of Rome. Imploding on its own sloth and waste. He just didn't know if that would be a good thing or not.

Rashid sighed and pulled the binoculars back to his face. His weary eyes continuing to scan the peaceful flowing river. Yes, another long night indeed.

Major Jack Sterling - commander of five man D company from the third battalion Rangers out of Fort Benning - floated peacefully along, making every effort to not cause any ripples. The water from the Tigris was warm and slow moving and ripples could be easily spotted. Sterling slowly lowered his head into the water - adjusted his night vision goggles - and raised his head back to the surface.

A shadow passed overhead and Jack could see the dark outline of the Jumariyah Bridge high above them. A small amount of traffic could be heard even from this distance. A large island was visible in the distance and his team diverted around the east side of it.

As the men rounded the crest of the island, a smaller island appeared just a bit further downstream; their destination. As the small island grew closer, they could make out the blue dome of the Republican Palace rising a short distance away. The searchlights were bright as they lit up the night sky; the surrounding grounds were a virtual beehive of activity.

Sterling would be glad to be out of the water. They had entered the river several miles north of the city - just after dusk - and had been floating for more than an hour with the gentle current. The river wasn't deep in most places and it took a good amount of effort to stay submerged and not become bogged down in the sandy bottom. The river had deepened as they entered Baghdad city proper making the going a little easier, but Sterling felt vulnerable in the river and dry land could not arrive soon enough.

He peered through his goggles at the rest of his team:

Second Lieutenant, Lance Duncan was right next to him - slowly drifting with the current. Expertly making subtle moves that would steer him to their island destination.

Duncan was the youngest member of the team - recently assigned. Sterling had figured that the young man could not have been cutting his teeth on a more difficult mission. He wasn't happy about a rookie being assigned to his watch for such a high level mission. But with the loss of one of his team in a recent training mishap, Duncan was next in line for the assignment. He had tested high in aptitude and marksmanship and the powers that be thought he had what it took. But Sterling wasn't so sure of their assessment and had decided to hold Duncan next to his waist and watch him. The young Lieutenant was already showing signs of impetuous behavior and Sterling's goal was to break him of this.

Several yards ahead, First Lieutenant Benjamin "Specs" Jacobs was slowly emerging from the water onto the sandy shoreline of the small island. He crouched behind a large boulder that hid him from view of the palace grounds. Jacobs was Jack Sterling's second in command and a master at taking point. His team had nicknamed him "Specs" for his uncanny ability at scouting and target spotting - his overly large eyes no small contributing factor. Specs looked like a giant black crab as he sidled away from the water's edge.

Behind Jacobs, Second Lieutenant Neal Anderson and Second Lieutenant Don Swanson were slow in emerging. Laying prone - half in and half out of the water - they trained their AK47's on the underbrush ahead of Specs.

From the water, Jack Sterling focused his night vision on the Republican Palace grounds. The grounds lay a mere fifty yards to their west. Searchlights were ablaze sweeping the river with scissor-like motions. Sterling could see that at least half a dozen other searchlights were pointed into the night sky in an attempt to block the prying eyes of American technology.

Radio silence was in force, but the small hand signals from Specs told him that it was safe to proceed onto the small land mass. The team made their way from the shores edge and settled in under some dense brush. They began an accounting of their equipment while attacking the difficult job of stripping themselves of their wet suits. The recon on the Republican Palace was not due for another night and they were in for a long hot day under the brutal Iraqi sun.

"So, that's it?" Duncan asked - his tone laced with excitement.

Sterling stared across the river to the large imposing building that rose above the not too distant shore. The Republican Palace, built in the 1950's for the last King of Iraq - Faisal II, was an impressive display to be sure. Rising to a height of thirty feet in most places, its central body stretched higher to apex at an impressive turquoise dome. The large, blue dome offered a splash of splendid color to an otherwise tan surrounding. The palace was the quintessence of opulence.

Saddam Hussein had held on to his power - with permission from the United States - as a stabilizing force in the region. But after Nine-Eleven, the stepped up surveillance and intercepted transmissions had shown that high level al-Qaeda and Hezbollah members were meeting - and possibly plotting further terrorist attacks on American soil. If true, then Saddam Hussein was no longer an asset to the United States and therefore his reign was likely to come to a quick end. Aside from desiring the good will of the Iraqi people, the war on terror needed a land base to operate from within the Middle-East. And if Saddam had gone rouge, it offered the United States a perfect opportunity. Intelligence chatter had indicated that a high level meeting was set for the next evening, and Sterling's team was there to confirm who was in attendance for the affair.

Sterling sighed quietly. "That's it, kid."

Sterling slid the chamber open on his nine millimeter, clicking a round home. Duncan continued to stare across the water to the mansion that rose massive in the night sky. Its façade backlit amongst the dozen or more searchlights that swung heavy arcs in all directions. "Get some rest, kid," Sterling said - interrupting the young sergeants daydream. "You can see it up close and personal tomorrow."

Duncan dropped his gaze. "Yes sir," he said somewhat reluctantly.

Sterling looked at the young man so recently assigned to him before letting his own gaze drift to the immense structure.

It did look opposing.

Intimidating.

A bad feeling suddenly began to gnaw its way through his stomach.

four

Brooklyn, New York; c. 1970's

Are we ready, Scott?" *Mr. Annoying* asked - raising the microphone closer to his mouth.

Dan Scott stepped behind the camera and reached into the news van for his headphones - ignoring the question. *Mr. Annoying* - known to the rest of the world as Rodney Jacobs - had asked that same question at least half a dozen times. And each time he had received the same response - *"I will let you know."*

Dan Scott was tired of repeating himself. He was also tired of this self-deluded blow-hard calling him by his last name because he thought it was his first name. Perhaps he was tired enough to start thinking of a different career path.

Scott didn't care much for field reporters; he considered most of them metro-sexual pansies with far too small a brain, a dick, and a paycheck for the size of the egos they carried with them. It never seemed to change either and he had worked with the best of them. This one though, seemed to have a special place in Dan Scott's book of the supremely, fucking annoying - *D'où le surnom.*

Dan Scott pulled the headphones over his ears, making sure he was receiving a signal from the station. *Wink Batton* - the station's news anchor - was beginning to tease their story, just ahead of the next series of commercials and Scott happily listened to the advertisements. So much the better the fringe benefit of blocking out the sound of *Mr.*

Annoying - who was still gesticulating wildly at him. Rain had been falling steadily for the last few minutes and the pain of watching this man trying to avoid the drops as if they were acid, was wearing on his nerves.

He let a sigh escape heavily through his puffed cheeks. Who was he kidding? A different career path?

Not likely.

Even though Dan Scott rarely played well with his colleagues, he did enjoy the work. Racing to scenes of devastation or tragedy; witnessing first-hand the heartbreak and misfortune that occasionally befell his fellow man. Capturing those moments on film in the hope to - one day - be the creator of that next iconic image that would embed itself in timeless Americana. Moments that captured humanity in its truest and rawest form - such as the kiss between the Sailor and Nurse in Times-Square at the end of World War Two, or the flag raising at Iwo-Jima.

Scott sighed again - shallower this time - as he looked through the camera lens at *Mr. Annoying* who had decided to entertain himself by doing ridiculous lip exercises; blowing through his pursed lips like a mutant horse. How could he expect his own creativity to flourish if he spent all of his time filming self important *wanna-be's* in Brooklyn? But what other options did he have? So another gas explosion happened. Big deal. The damage wasn't that bad. He would never get his award winning photograph here. Where was the anguish?

The sorrow?

Scott shook his head in silence - maybe someday. But for now, if he didn't get *Mr. Annoying on* camera - and on time - he'd be getting a tongue lashing tomorrow morning by the boss. And that didn't fit well with the hangover he planned on having.

The commercials had ended - it was time. Raising his fingers to signal the countdown, he tried to ignore the radiant, teeth filled smile that flashed into the camera.

Three

Two

One...

Scott pointed as the light on the camera indicated tape was rolling.

"Thanks, Wink. This is Rodney Jacobs," the smile said. "Reporting live at the scene of what is being called an explosion, that rocked this small neighborhood near the Park Slope area at Lincoln and Seventh avenue mere moments ago."

Scott panned the camera back over Jacobs' shoulder, relieved that he could take the focus away from that specious smile. *"What is being called an explosion?"* Oh God, he hated this man! *What the hell else would you call it?* The camera lens focused on the remains of the café in the early morning gloom.

Mr. Annoying continued preening to his adoring, if not imaginary fan base, "The explosion occurred close to midnight at this little cafe behind me - *'The Heart of Brooklyn.'* Witnesses on the scene state that at least three people detonated devices that must have been strapped to their persons..."

To the bystanders inside and outside of the little café in downtown Brooklyn in 1972, the fact that the explosion was technically an *implosion* meant little; the effect was the same. The violent disintegration of the large plate glass window had flung tables, booths and thousands of pieces of fragmented glass into the street and throughout the eatery. And with only one death - which seemed to be unrelated - no one appeared to have been seriously hurt by the incident.

No detonation device was located. The three men that had been at the source of the violence had mysteriously disappeared; remains of them were never found. And although witnesses to the events of that evening inside the little café swore they saw three men - and each were consistent in their description of them - the lack of evidence of their existence made their inclusion in the official report too wildly contradictory as to remain.

Dan Scott brought his camera back to *Mr. Annoying.*

Jacobs' microphone had found - and was hovering in front of - the face of a young, provocatively dressed woman:

"Yeah, I saw them," she slurred. "One of them had a beard and torn up clothes. I think he was black. He must have been a hobo *cuz* I could smell him from across the room. I think the other guys were feeding him - out of kindness, *dig*? But they all seemed rather chummy. The good looking guys called the hobo, *Doc.* Anyway the hobo ate - and I mean a lot. He couldn't shovel the food in fast enough. But when the cops came in, they all blew up. But it wasn't a huge explosion, *you dig*? It was more like a huge gust of wind. Kind of like when the windows blew out of my house during a tornado when I was kid. Kind of like that..."

The only fatality of the evening was that of a young woman who had crumpled just outside of the restaurant. Official autopsy reports would eventually show she had been suffering from a recently diagnosed brain aneurism that had ruptured during the excitement of the evening. Her case appeared altogether unrelated to the events that had occurred inside the café and was only included as a small footnote in the official report.

If Dan Scott was looking for anguish that night, he need only have brought his camera slightly south of the café entrance.

To Larimer Leopold Lownsbury - former professor of history, reluctant time traveler and one third of the reason for the destruction of the little café that had just occurred - the memories flooded back. The vision of his mother as she had walked into the café and those precious last few minutes that he had had with her. Even the little things like the taste of the grilled cheese and the sweetness of that rare cola he was allowed. How he had taken those minutes for granted. He wished he could have had those minutes back.

Lownsbury's eyes welled as he watched from across the street - his mother and himself as a ten year old boy, walk calmly away from the destroyed restaurant. Sirens floated into existence in the distance as he saw his mother fall to the sidewalk. The look of concern emblazoned upon his younger self's face was unmistakable - even from this distance.

Oh God, how could he bear to watch this again?

He thought that he could, but this was too much.

Lownsbury found himself running across the street towards them. His heart and voice as one, catching in his throat - a scream transforming to a horsy croak, *"Momma!"*

Reaching down next to his younger self, Lownsbury held his mother's head aloft so both of them could look upon her. His mind reeled as he remembered this very incident occurring. How odd that it seemed so natural a thing, even back then. A stranger, reaching from the dark - both of them sharing their grief. Both experiencing this fresh born nightmare. Yet the younger unaware that the strange, disheveled man that wept with him would be his future self.

Lownsbury's tears cut paths through the grime on his face as his mother opened her eyes. That familiar smile - like a light from heaven - beamed at him as she saw the man her son was to become. He could see the recognition in her eyes.

She knew him! Even through his tousled and gaunt exterior, *she knew him!*

Bringing her hand to his cheek, her last words - although quiet - thundered in his ears, *"My Larimer."*

And then she was gone.

✔ive

Waset, Kemet - (Thebes, Egypt); c. 1550 BCE

Pen-Nekhbet; newly appointed **Royal Herald and Seal Bearer;** in service to the royal family of Ah-Mose and the living god and king - Seqenenre Tao - gazed in astonishment around the room in which he waited.

He considered himself an artisan of the highest caliber; the top of his class in crafting records of flawless accuracy. And of course, he had been witness to many of the works of artistic mastery of his predecessors. Yet he now stood in absolute awe at the display of grandeur that accented this palace room and - in fact - the entire area. The opulence of this room compared to his own quarters was glaringly vivid - punctuated by the numerous colored glyphs that adorned the walls. Flawless graffito that conveyed grand stories of the royal house of Ah-Mose.

Pen-Nekhbet read easily through the pictured sagas, including impressive accounts of military conquests and the delightful tales of the many births of sons and of daughters. There was also the story of the family's ascension to the throne, as well as dozens of other anecdotal narratives on the pleasure of the gods that looked favorably upon the royal family of Ah-Mose: *The Child of the Moon*. It was an enchanting embellishment of a house that had stretched back through many generations and seemed poised to continue.

Pen-Nekhbet ran his hand lovingly over the familiar glyph of his and his township's namesake and patron goddess; Nekhbet: *The Mother of Mothers.* The beautiful goddess - adorned in colorful vulture feathers - was an exquisite piece of work. The blending of gold and turquoise the artist had used was outstanding. Her wings outstretched - conveying comfort as she knelt in front of the first family patriarch - fully captured the feeling of maternity and love for the family.

Beyond the magnificent, gold laced tapestry, Pen-Nekhbet could see outside to the great courtyard - replete with trees hanging heavy with fruit. The green leaves of the garden were dazzling under the hot Egyptian sun. Every inch of the grand room and its opulent garden reminded him of the benefits of royalty and his own place among them.

His own place.

Pen-Nekhbet rubbed the heavy cylinder of the royal seal - that hung from a gold chain around his neck - through the fingers of his right hand. Carefully, so as not to remove it. He smiled as he remembered fondly the events of the previous evening and how his personal position in the palace had improved greatly:

The palace had thrown a massive Heb Sed gala, to honor king Seqenenre Tao's upcoming diplomatic visit north to Avaris - and the honorary coronation of the joining of Upper and Lower Egypt with his crowning of the *Sekhemty*; The crown of the two lands.

The *Heb Sed* festival was traditionally held for just such extraordinary events, as well as the opportunity to showcase courtier advancements throughout the palace. The celebrations would likely continue for the next several evenings, but the first night was the one that was most significant for Pen-Nekhbet. And the one that had changed his life forever:

The palace had been host that evening to governors and officials from every township and territory of Upper Egypt, each turning out to get face time with his majesty. Each wanting a piece of the credit for the final unification of Egypt. And each looking to feather his own bed with profit to be made from the launching of any bold new enterprise from the evening's festivities. It was certain to be an historic event, Pen-Nekhbet had thought. The peace talks between the two kings of Upper and Lower Egypt were destined to enter the annals of history as a monumental turning point between the two lands.

At least that was the current propaganda espoused.

Pen-Nekhbet was not naive in regard to political propaganda by any means. He was surrounded with it every day with his work inside the palace. He could hear political speak in his dreams and could certainly recognize it during his waking time.

But on this night, the dictates of the palace were not his to question and the opening night of his first *Heb Sed* was one to be remembered fondly - not one to be squandered with political cynicism.

His own place.

Thinking back, Pen-Nekhbet's recent rise in rank had been a sudden and double edged surprise when his friend - and the palace's lead scribe, *Hornakht* - had unexpectedly died that previous season. Hornakht's death had created an opening for the lead scribe position and Pen-Nekhbet - having seniority - had been immediately promoted. A modest advancement, but admittedly not one that warranted an invitation to a *Heb Sed*.

As new head scribe though, his next step in accession was that of Royal Herald. And with a surprising endorsement from Prince Ka-Mose - via the invitation to the palace for opening night of the *Heb Sed* - Pen-Nekhbet's advancement to Royal Herald had suddenly been made official. As befitting his rank, he would be named at the *Heb Sed* as an honorary member of the royal family of Ah-Mose; a privilege of the highest order.

The blessings of *Ah-Mun* had certainly been looking favorably upon him, he had thought.

Pen-Nekhbet knew that the *Sed* Festival was the designated venue for all courtier advancements. But he was also well aware that the promotion would remain unofficial until the following morning - after the gala. Thus was the case with all promotions across the court. Even the king himself was among those destined to advance with his crowning of the *Sekhemty*; the coveted crown of the two lands of Egypt. A ceremony signifying the unification of Lower and Upper Egypt with the formal ritual performed by none other than the high priest, *Ah-Mun*.

Yes, the evening was destined to be magical and memorable.

Enchanting music - played by the finest musicians in all of Egypt - reverberated through the massive hall as Pen-Nekhbet made his way to the banquet tables for the third time. The wine and beer were flowing like red and gold rivers and the food was so deliciously prepared that he thought he would burst - unable and unwilling to fight his gluttony.

The tables boasted the finest, fresh roasted meat including beef, goat and mutton. There were heaping dishes of grilled fish - caught that very morning from the Black river - alongside massive platters stacked with goose, pigeon, duck, heron and crane - sizzling succulently under copper chafing dishes. A variety of vegetables including onions, leeks, garlic, radishes and turnips, swimming in specialty sauces with mouthwatering flavors of cumin, coriander, sesame, dill and fennel were offered. Scattered throughout the dining hall were platters of dates, figs, plums and melons that could be easily reached for a quick, sweet dessert.

Beer was a staple of every Egyptian household and growing up, Pen-Nekhbet's home had been no exception. He was quite familiar with the honeyed barley flavor of his favorite beverage mash, but tonight he decided he would have his fill of wine instead - more of an indulgent delicacy befitting a night such as this. The serving staff filled Pen-Nekhbet's mug to the brim with the rosy liquid, causing him to have a gentle hand as he brought the mug to his lips.

From the corner of his eye, Pen-Nekhbet spied a lone figure. Clad in a long, dark, hooded cloak. The person stood rock still, purposefully distant from the crowd. The cloak concealed the persons face entirely. Even though he was unable to see the person's eyes, Pen-Nekhbet had the unmistakable feeling that *he* was the sole focus of the mysterious person's attention.

The presence was unnerving and the need to investigate proved overwhelming. Pen-Nekhbet began crossing the span of the palace floor to approach the cloaked figure. But by the time he managed to break free from the crowd, the person was no longer there. Vanished amidst the mass of people congregating throughout the great hall.

How eerily odd, Pen-Nekhbet thought - running the image of the figure through his mind.

Shaking his head in resignation, he sipped at his mug of wine - wincing at its spicy sweetness - heavily exhaling its heady aftertaste. Eying a bowl of dates that adorned a nearby table he helped himself to one of the large pieces of the tasty fruit. The bitter fruit contrasted sharply with the sugary wine, over sensitizing his palate.

"Ugh!" he grimaced.

Spitting the remains of the partially masticated fruit into a nearby bin, Pen-Nekhbet attempted to cleanse the flavor from his mouth with another gulp of wine and a sharp inhale.

"That was a mistake," A voice next to him sang mirthfully.

Startled, Pen-Nekhbet turned to see a young palace girl smiling playfully at him. "Wine and dates often make for poor bedfellows. At least to the untrained palate. My name is Ipu," she said sweetly - holding her hand out to him displaying the lack of jewelry or ink on her delicate fingers.

The statement was clear; she was not married or betrothed and her approach to him was one of intrigue. She was offering a gentle invitation to converse and Pen-Nekhbet was inclined to respond as part of custom and etiquette.

He smiled. Perhaps this gala *was* to be an evening fondly remembered, he thought - pushing the mysterious cloaked figure from his mind.

Six

Baghdad, Iraq; 2002

Separated only by a small grove of orange trees, the rear of the Republican Palace faced the Tigris River in which Sterling's team had assembled - just offshore. The Republican Guard that patrolled the palace appeared to be out in full force, which only seemed to confirm the intelligence reports that a high level meeting was set to take place that evening.

Major Jack Sterling pulled a pair of field glasses to his eyes and watched as a Republican Guardsman - high atop a guard post - lowered his own binoculars to light a cigarette. This shouldn't be too difficult, he considered. A quick insertion and extraction and a few clandestine photographs of who was in attendance.

Sterling smiled, '*a walk in the park.*'

But that knot in his stomach persisted.

Silent and wraithlike, Major Jack Sterling and his Rangers pulled themselves from the river onto the sandy shore that lay behind Saddam Hussein's Presidential Republican Palace. Under the cover of the orange and palm trees that surrounded the palace grounds, they split up to each team's respective positions.

Sterling and Duncan cut south across the grove, to the far end of the compound. Anderson and Swanson began their trek to the north side of the building as Specs made his way alone to the front side of the palace to monitor who was arriving.

The palace was lit up like a gala event; its turquoise dome looked like a big blue marble, shining under the magnificent illumination. Four massive searchlights streaked across the heavens in a futile attempt to disrupt any cameras that may be looking down onto the palace grounds.

The teams were silent as they wound their way through and around orange trees, massive palms and small buildings that occupied the palace grounds. Their gear; noiseless - strapped securely to their bodies as they inched closer to the back side of the structure.

Sterling and Duncan reached the outer edge of the orange grove and peered through the thicket of foliage at the rear of the palace. A large swimming pool was lit up and squeals of laughter could be heard amidst splashing. Six young girls were giggling and laughing as they relaxed and swam in the chlorinated water. They were the palace harem, blowing off steam before they were called into service later that evening.

'Specs' slid around the north wing of the palace and snuggled into position behind a small grouping of trees that offered a perfect view of the roundabout drive at the palace front. He pulled a small handheld tablet from his gear and uplinked to a satellite in geosynchronous orbit above them. The searchlights did nothing to hinder the satellites operation and within seconds, a crystal clear view of the palace grounds materialized on the small screen.

The earpiece in Sterling's ear came alive with a small whispered statement from Jacobs, "Spec's online."

"Alpha Copy," Sterling stated simply.

The teams held silent for several seconds until Jacobs's whispered voice once again sounded, "We have three, two man teams of RG's patrolling the grounds," he said - indicating the Royal Guard. "One RG team is very close to Alpha's five. Another near the barracks in the rear and another at Bravo's two."

Sterling and Duncan scanned their five o'clock position and could see a flicker of movement through the trees.

"The girls are a magnet, we need to move," Sterling whispered in Duncan's ear.

"We have visitors in the drive," Specs said - a short pause - then, "It's the 'S' man, or a DG. Heavily surrounded. Making his way in."

"Copy," Sterling answered. Saddam Hussein or one of his lookalikes had arrived. The lookalikes were referred to as DG's - a code name for Doppelganger.

"Another limo just pulled up. Oh sweet Jesus, its OBL! As I shit and breathe! Wow Mage, we got high level shit going on here!"

"I need a confirmation on that. OBL is on sight?" Sterling shot back. "We gotta be golden on this one, Specs."

"You got platinum, Mage. He be strutting his stuff. A whole entourage wrapping him up."

"We need to get inside," Sterling said. "We gotta find out what's going on."

"No prob, Mage. We got three teams of RG's, walking the perimeter, one coming up on your position now," Specs said - reading his camera positioning.

"Ok, let's make this quiet. Duncan you track left, *tranks* only. Clean and still and out of sight."

Sterling and Duncan performed the maneuvers efficiently. Each putting a fast acting tranquilizer dart into both guards. They were unconscious before their knees buckled under the weight of their torsos.

Stealing a radio from one of the guards, Sterling slipped the earpiece into his left ear. His right ear still receiving signals from Specs.

"Bravo, you have a two man team coming in on your left," Specs said again.

A brief tussle was heard over the *comm.* and then Anderson gave the all clear, "The sandman cometh."

"Copy."

Major Sterling looked at Duncan, "Slow and quiet, we go in. Follow my lead."

Duncan followed Sterling, gracefully slipping unobserved around the pool. The girls were far too preoccupied to notice them. Quietly, they crept into the open bath house door that led into the palace ground interior.

"Indoors, I repeat, Alpha is indoors," Duncan reported.

"Copy that Alpha," Specs replied.

Radio silence ensued as Sterling and Duncan made their way through the posh corridors. Sterling had memorized the floor plans to the palace and knew where the main meeting room was situated.

Suddenly Sterling's left ear was alive with Arabic chatter.

"RG is wanting to know the status of their perimeter guards," Sterling whispered into his comm. "We are now on countdown, 7 minutes - I repeat - 7 minutes."

Seven

Brooklyn, New York; c. 1970's

Larimer Lownsbury knew someone was there, even before he felt the touch upon his shoulder. But his mind did not - could not - at that moment, grasp the significance of the stranger's first word - "*Larimer?*"

Lownsbury raised his head and looked at the man through bleary eyes. It was raining and the water blended with the tears that ran openly down his emaciated cheeks. The stranger's face was familiar, yet distant.

"Larimer?" The man again said gently, "Leave the boy to me, you know he will be safe. You have to go now."

Lownsbury's mind struggled to coherency, "You know my name? Who are you?"

"You have to go," the stranger repeated - pulling the dejected man to his feet.

Lownsbury looked back to the dead woman and the weeping child. The boy's despondent cries of, "*Momma! Please, momma!*" echoed amongst the neighborhood buildings and became lost throughout the rapidly filling street.

"Larimer! You have to go!" The stranger was insistent.

Lownsbury wiped the tears from his eyes with the sleeve of his grimy, torn, sports coat. His mind jumped back and forth between the question of how this stranger knew him and merely accepting the fact that he did. Misery still plagued his soul and it took everything he had to peel himself away from this sad memory of his former life.

"You should not have come here," the stranger continued - pulling at his arm. "It is a risk you cannot afford."

Lownsbury noted absently that the insistent stranger was big, but not overweight. He wore an army fatigue jacket that only accentuated his size. Lownsbury could make out sandy blonde hair worn almost to shoulder length in the dim street light. He placed the man in his late thirty's. Without a handsome face - a long scar ran nearly the full length of his left cheek starting under his eye and ending just under his ear.

"Hal?" Lownsbury recalled. He knew this man. A kind man that had watched after him as a boy the night his mother had died.

His mother.

The re-acquainted stranger was right. He should not have come here.

When Captain Jack Sterling had insisted that Lownsbury pick a place in time in which the three of them - himself, Will Masters and Sterling - could go to reconnoiter, this was the first place that had come to mind. Perhaps it was an unconscious effort to see his beloved mother for the last time.

But he was down-at-heel. It had been months since his last bath. His stay in prison for witchcraft in old Salem Village had worn him to a frazzle. An unwashed and overgrown mass of hair and beard teemed with lice. His teeth and gums were in desperate need of reacquainting with a toothbrush. And he had serious doubts a single bar of soap could clean away the months of grunge that had accumulated from the miserable, New England dungeon in which he had been residing.

Choosing this place - at this time - had been a mistake. A mistake that could endanger his team and his loved ones - past and present. But it was an even bigger mistake hanging around to witness - once again - this miserable moment. He needed to get away from here.

"Go Larimer," The man insisted with much more urgency.

"Hal? How did you know it was me? How can you know that I..."

"Larimer!" Hal cut him off sharply, "Get the hell out of here, now! We will talk again one day, but for now - *leave!*"

People were beginning to filter towards them to see what kind of distress the despondent young child was in with the wake of the café explosion. Questions were already coming from members of the crowd.

"Hey, you guys. What's going on?"

"We can talk later Larimer," Hal repeated with finality. "You have to go!"

Hal forcibly began to shove Lownsbury towards an alley. Bringing his face close to Lownsbury's ear - he whispered, "Be very careful who you trust and don't make this kind of mistake again!"

Breaking from Lownsbury, Hal turned to handle the mass of people that were congregating.

A news van pulled up, nearly blocking the intersection. Lownsbury could hear police sirens closing in. His final view was that of Hal, pulling ten year old Larimer from his mother's side. Hands of gentle consolation wrapping him up.

Dazed, Lownsbury turned down the alley. Stumbling along, he pulled a small device - held together with a grimy handkerchief - from his only intact outer coat pocket.

But where would he go?

Captain Sterling had insisted that he fade into anonymity; living the rest of his life in obscure mediocrity. But where would that be? He could go anywhere to anytime in history, but he had no clue where.

The decision to leap into time with Samantha Moon - Senator Schulte's maniacal daughter - in order to save his team, had turned into an agonizing disaster resulting in his imprisonment for witchcraft in Salem Village, Massachusetts. During his escape from Salem, he had been forced to leave Samantha behind; abandoning her to her fate in a New England dungeon. Now he wanted nothing more than to return to his own time - his own life. But that was over. Fading into obscurity as Captain Sterling had wanted him to do, suddenly seemed a daunting task.

But daunting task or not, it did seem undeniable providence at that moment. His career was over; his colleagues at the university would be happy to never see his return. His family was gone; his ex-wife couldn't care less if he was alive or dead. Aside from the familial bond he had created with William Masters and Captain Sterling, he had ties to no one. His grief rose anew. He stumbled, a slight moan escaped him as he pushed his angst aside.

One thing was certain - before deciding on anything else, he desperately needed to clean himself up.

But where could he go to accomplish even this?

An idea came to him, but he discarded it as dangerous and merely justification for his own desires.

The idea persisted.

It was possible, but he had to be extremely careful. The slightest mistake - even being seen - could lead to disaster on a massive scale. He had underestimated Senator Schulte before, he could not afford to do it again. It was paramount that the senator remain in the dark about the location of his daughter. Lownsbury was the only person in the world who knew of her true location and he intended to keep it that way. He could not afford even the slightest mistake.

Entering the coordinates into the device, he pressed the button. A sizzling arc of electricity snapped through the atmosphere followed by a sharp crack as collapsing air filled the void that had so recently been occupied by Professor Larimer Lownsbury.

Eight

Baghdad, Iraq; 2002

Sterling and Duncan huddled next to each other inside a small office. The room was dark and empty and adjoined a large meeting room where the attendees had gathered. A massive, hand carved door separated the rooms.

Pulling various pieces of equipment from their packs, Duncan slipped a small whip camera under the door. A clear color picture came to life on the hand held device. Unfortunately, the tip of the camera came up next to the boot of an attending guard so a portion of the room could not be seen. A chip sized microphone connected to the flexible camera recorded the conversation.

Most of the men were speaking in Arabic, but Sterling was able to translate.

"The Americans are mobilizing for war." - Sterling believed the voice as that belonging to Bin Laden - "You assured us that this would not be the case."

"As I mentioned, the original plan involved Charles Hicks winning the election," an unseen voice replied in English. Sterling did not immediately recognize the owner, but an arrogant inflection was unmistakable - he sounded familiar. Very familiar. "Since Thomas Bishop won the presidential office, we need to curb our plans for attacks on American soil. You should have heeded my warning and delayed the heavy plane assault for a few more years. You have virtually guaranteed him a second term."

"We cannot dictate Allah's will, nor question his motives," OBL again. "His will be done."

"And does Allah sanction the United States' targeting of Iraq?" Unseen voice again, "I can stifle President Bishop for a short amount of time, but you must get your weapons out of this country."

"I do not fear the Americans," Saddam Hussein boasted. "Allah will provide. We have assets spread all through America. Bishop would not dare strike here."

"You have ignited the passion of the American people, Mr. President. They will want both of your heads and in a very short time frame. Make no mistake, they will be coming."

"Then you must prevent him from doing so," Saddam replied.

"Even my resources are limited," Mr. Unknown said - calmly. "Until we have Hicks in office, the American war machine will certainly roll through the Middle East. Starting here in Iraq. We will have to wait until we have attained the presidency to loosen any grip. Perhaps we can insist on a predetermined time frame for withdrawal. But nonetheless, we must be patient. I have a plan taking shape. But you must stop your saber rattling and hide those weapons. And both of you must go into exile."

"We will not hide like beaten dogs," OBL sneered. "Americans will soon realize that Allah will no longer suffer their existence. The United States will turn red with its people's decadent blood. And we will stand victorious on a mountain of their dead."

"Of course," Mr. Unknown seemed to smile - though his demeanor radiated command. "But you will cease your impetuousness, or you shall certainly unravel all of our plans."

Just as Sterling was contemplating what kind of plans could be in the making, his earpiece erupted. "Shit, Major!" It was Specs and his voice was tense - unnerved, "We've been compromised!"

There was a large amount of scuffle and the unmistakable rattle of gunfire could be heard outside the palace walls. Moving away from the door that separated him and Duncan from the meeting room, Sterling spoke in a hushed whisper into his communication system, "Specs! Report! ... Bravo! ... Bravo, Report! ... *Shit*!" Turning to the young sergeant - he ordered, "Duncan, abort. We need to get out of here!"

Duncan was standing, a slight smile crossing his face. "I don't think so, Major." In his hand he held his sidearm pointed directly at Sterling's head.

"Duncan!" Sterling hissed - his eyes locked on the younger man. "What the hell are you doing?"

"Just following orders, sir."

After forcing Sterling to disarm, Duncan reached behind his back and gave five rhythmic knocks on the massive door. His eyes and weapon still trained on Sterling, he found the knob and pulled the big door open. Gesturing with his head, Duncan steered a disbelieving Sterling into the opulent meeting room.

Nine

Somewhere In The Rocky Mountains;

Date: Unknown

The house, though exquisite, lay invisible. Forgotten. Relegated to the annals of myth and legend.

Sitting high against a rough, sloping peak deep within the White River National Forest in Colorado - and nestled within a blanket of green pines, blue spruce and white trunked aspens - the home radiated the opulence of a peaceful, mountain getaway. Massive windows surrounded most of the home and offered a one hundred and eighty degree view of the spectacular Rocky Mountain Range. The cathedral style roof peaks blended well with the scenery - providing further camouflage to any daring soul that was able to venture close enough.

Covered in snow nine months of the year, the home featured sheer drops into jagged rocks along three sides. A forest - impenetrable by vehicle along its remaining side - had made traditional access to the home impossible. The property was surrounded by wire fencing and topped with a continuous spool of barbed wire - the ubiquitous '*No Hunting*' sign strewn hither and yonder. The fence encircled the property's three dozen, tree lined acres - leaving no visible evidence that a home lay at its center.

A house that time had forgotten.

And while the occasional hunter would stumble upon the property line from time to time, very few would dare cross the wired boundary.

The legend of the *'Dark Man'* kept most of the local curiosity seekers away. Those unfamiliar with the epic tale of the *'Dark Man'* that did decide to brave the crossing, never returned to confirm or deny this specter's shadowy existence.

The myth of a giant demon that patrolled the grounds - dressed in a long black coat and hat, his face and eyes the color of pitch and with hands the size of catchers mitts - was as old as time. The ancient legend of a cannibalistic monster of enormous strength that would eviscerate trespassers, had been passed down from generation to generation through the Ute Indian tribes of the area. The American settlers had further embroidered the tale through the years with fabrications and rumors - each more fanciful than the last. And every subsequent recounting seemed to be laced with escalated tales of unspeakable horror and fantastic feats of bravery from the teller.

Nobody knew when the mysterious home that surrounded this *'Dark Man'* saga was built - it had always just been rumored to be there. No local could ever be found that had ever been to the home - much less seen it - and its inexplicable presence only served to augment the legend.

To Senator Theodore Godescalcus Schulte, the mysterious home was his personal, private retreat. His own fortress of solitude that could afford him the isolation he needed - far removed from the prying eyes of the rest of the world. The *'Dark Man'* legend served him well to those ends.

A gentle breeze wafted through the home and - as if by magic - Schulte appeared in the living room. His gate quick, his brow furrowed in perplexity. As was tradition, his first stop inside the home was to be made at a small liquor table that he kept along the far side. Situated opposite of the massive bay windows - but fully protected against contact with the sun's rays - the bar held the finest spirits money could buy.

He poured himself three fingers of *Marquis de Montesquiou* - an early vintage, Armagnac brandy - and downed the fiery liquid in a single throw. With a heavy exhale, he again touched the bottle to the rim of his glass.

Although far from a novice at time travel, he found the experience not without its side effects and brandy - especially fine brandy - had always been his preferred remedy at relieving the mild ailments.

He paused.

Somewhere within the penetralia of his opulent home, he could hear the terrified screaming of a young girl. Probably in her middle teens by the tone and inflection of the shriek, Schulte guessed. And with a smirk, he raised the glass to his lips for a soothing, lingering sip this time.

He listened for a moment longer - mildly distracted as the desperate, female cries reverberated hysterically through the mountain retreat. His pulse quickened as his ears captured the intonation of each pitiful wail - the echo moving up the staircase to the attic lofts above him. And then, out to the open air balcony overlooking the massive, rocky abyss below.

Schulte - in eager anticipation of what was to follow - made his way to the living room's large, bay window and cast his gaze to the balcony above. He could see his servant Dain, making his way out to the open decking - a young, naked girl held firmly under his left arm.

It mattered little from where, or even when the girl came. Nor even what her name was. She had been used as a donor for one of his daughter's rejuvenation processes. Dain had certainly acquired her in some distant past, as he did all of his children's donors. Likely deemed a runaway or a lost cause, she had long ago become a soul forgotten; an indifferent name in the annals of some past life. And now - with the girl's *essence* having been absorbed into Samantha - she was a mindless, soulless creature to be discarded.

Schulte watched, transfixed.

Some may have called it a macabre fancy, or perhaps a singular, ghoulish curiosity but Schulte always enjoyed witnessing this unfolding drama when he had the good fortune to be here for it. His heart rate quickened in anticipation as he endeavored to capture every heart pounding moment of this unfortunate girls final seconds. Throwing open a window, a chilling mountain breeze removed every trace of warmth from the room but it brought with it every sound, every scent, every pulse pounding second of the balcony drama unfolding. The girl's shrieking wail echoed through the mountain canyon - bouncing in perfect reverberation through the narrow pass and Schulte instinctually became aroused. Her frantic, terrified cry reached a caustic pitch as she realized what was about to happen and Schulte basked in that heightened terror.

He could feel his blood coursing hard through his veins, his heart pounding in his chest as beads of sweat erupted from his pores. His breathing quickened as he watched her struggle. She was so alive, so desperate, so frenzied with a tidal wave of emotion that poured from her. He could sense her helplessness; knowing there was nothing she could do about her impending doom. A small spittle of drool gathered at the corner of his mouth as he watched. His excitement mounted as Dain effortlessly lifted the helpless young girl above his head.

Unconsciously, Schulte rubbed the fingertips of his free hand together. His eyes wide - his pupils dilated in anticipation. He could feel his breath catch even further as he watched the vertigo sluice through the young girl's body at the sight of the yawning chasm that opened up below her. An acrid odor erupted into the air as her bladder released. The liquid flowed into the open air. Tears cascaded heavily from her eyes and she began to shake uncontrollably. Realizing she had only seconds to live, she grabbed beseechingly at Dain's immense arms - her fingers desperately searching for any purchase to prevent the inevitable.

Schulte's nostrils flared, catching her scent. The fear was radiating from her in musky waves. His every sense was alive and he nearly cried out in delight when Dain launched her high into the air. Her screaming intensified as their eyes met and Schulte could see every nuance of horror dancing across her face as she sailed, helpless in her freefall.

Caught in the whirlwind Doppler Effect, the cadence and intonation of her scream changed as she flew by the massive living room window - becoming abruptly silenced by her body's sudden, brutal impact onto the jagged rocks below. An ebullition of red and white erupted from the force of the collision, shredding her as she tumbled with inhuman movement across the jagged points.

Finally, she would come to rest - tangled in a rocky outcropping or in the branches of the snow capped forest canopy. Her remains left to await the ineluctable, prowling, nocturnal scavenger that would drag her corpse away and into the night.

Schulte let out another long, low, alcohol laced exhale. His own tantalization having peaked, his heart rate began to slow. He closed his eyes and shivered in the empty room as the young girl's body rolled out of sight to its inevitable end.

Finally - his afternoon diversion having ended - he slowly lowered the sash. The chill mountain air that had violated the living room immediately began to yield to the insistence of the home's heating system.

It was an exhilarating feeling watching the young girls drop by the window - their bodies floundering helplessly in mid-air. The viciousness of the slayings and the desperation heard in the girls' final pleas, offered Schulte a strange dichotomy to the opulent peacefulness of his mountain surroundings.

But, it was so much more than that.

Extreme age seemed to lessen the normal emotional responses most people felt. And immortality - even more so. After so many years of living, even the excitement of sex had devolved into a prosaic pastime. Schulte had come to realize through the years that immortality created an emotional void that - at times - needed to be filled with the strong emotions of others. Samantha had her way of filling that need with her sexual sadism. Schulte's addiction was fed in a rather different way. And - as with any drug - a search endures for an ever increasing high. For Schulte, nothing projected that intensity of fury and fervor than young females about to die. Nothing satisfied that emotional vacuum more effectively than their terrified cries and abrupt terminal silence.

With the ability to travel through time as easily as walking through the room, Dain would hunt his children's donors across the span of time. Housing them in cages until their emotions peaked. And after their purpose was served, deliver unto them the greatest gift in life. The gift of their own mortality. A gift impossible for them to appreciate. A gift only an immortal could covet.

Schulte shivered as he relived the girl's death plummet. Would, that he ever experience that feeling of such finality? To taste and touch, to feel what lay on the other side? If there was still a God, surely that was where he resided. Was it so macabre to wish for death? To savor that ultimate release that his children's donors experienced at the height of their terror?

Schulte opened his eyes and turned. As expected, the *'Dark Man'* had appeared and was standing - immobile and mute - in the center of the living room. At nearly eight feet in height, the man was a giant. An enormous being with insurmountable strength. Swaddled in a black trench coat, a slightly tilted fedora partially concealed a horribly disfigured and age blackened face. Schulte's mother - ages ago had often said that to stare Dain directly in the face, was to invite a lifetime of nightmares to your sleep.

"Good afternoon, Dain," Schulte said quietly to the big man. "Thank you for that, but I'm afraid we will be needing another donor for my daughter."

And as was usual, there would be no reply.

Many times, Schulte would try in vain to recall if he could ever remember having heard the giant speak. There were just too many years to be able to remember. As was the norm, he shook his head in defeat.

Once a high priest of a long lost empire, Dain now served Schulte as keeper of his gate. Immortal and ancient, the *Dark Man* was a testament to the ravages of time; his skin and eyes as mottled and as blackened as his timeless soul.

His ability to move through time and space was unparalleled. Dain would appear motionless - as if fastened to the floor - suddenly fading, only to locate somewhere else. He appeared mostly as a shimmer now; a dark, spectral shimmer. An inhuman, ghostly statue that moved invisibly through the room. Folding time around him as easily as air moved around solid mass.

Keeping mostly to Schulte's mountain retreat when he wasn't hunting the children's rejuvenation donors through the ages, Dain would monitor the outer perimeter for trespassers. Very few, however ventured past the barbed fencing anymore. Such was the profundity of the *'Dark Man'* legend.

Taking his last swallow, Schulte moved toward the liquor table - only vaguely aware of Dain's ethereal movements behind him. A shimmering onyx statue, the giant solidified - remaining stock still - silently awaiting Schulte's command.

Schulte's thoughts were now elsewhere though.

He had become engrossed with a moderate sized jar sitting on a shelf within a small hutch in the far corner of the room. The jar was simply labeled *Kiya*, and contained a human heart. As if possessing a life force all its own, the heart pressed against the glass - beating in rhythmic harmony to his own. Each movement of the muscle mesmerizingly swirled the translucent, silver liquid in which it hung suspended. Each beat compelled his thoughts - guiding him through his reverie.

His reflections were swept to Samantha. His need to find her had become paramount. He was feeling the impact of her absence and he knew she must also be feeling the effects as well. His thinking was becoming clouded and his ability to concentrate was faltering. They had learned long ago not to venture more than a century away from each other - their recent estrangement was not the first in their long history together - but each time, he hoped it would prove to be their last.

Blinking and turning from the jar, he finished his pour and recapped the decorative decanter. They had been dealt a minor blow with this unexpected separation. An unfortunate turn of events that had stretched beyond the boundaries of annoying and was strumming magnificently at the tenuous fibers of his patience.

"Another small impediment to conquer," he said - a bit too effusively as he touched the fiery liquid to his lips. The oaky aroma steadied him and he closed his eyes as he cast his thoughts to the recent interrogation attempt he had undertaken with Will Masters. He was extremely disappointed - perhaps even a bit unnerved - that the boy had been unable to supply any information as to Samantha's whereabouts in spite of the liberal application of ant venom beneath the young man's fingernails.

He sighed heavily as he lowered his arm. The strong alcohol was having the intended effect.

Focus!

Masters had disclosed that it had been Professor Lownsbury who had managed to defeat Samantha, leaving her somewhere locked in time. And although Schulte had found it difficult to believe that the bumbling fool had found a way to overpower his daughter, he had also lived long enough to know that stranger things were possible.

The question before him now became: *Where to find the professor?*

"Dain," Schulte said - without looking back at the big man. "Pull Professor Lownsbury's file for me, would you please?"

There was not so much as a breeze, so masterful at time manipulation as the massive man was that by the time Schulte turned around, the file was being handed to him. He glanced through the pages as he paced. Dain again vanished, appearing on the other side of the room as if he were a ghost that inhabited the home.

Schulte was having a hard time concentrating on the pages, so he closed his eyes and stretched his neck. Lack of concentration had become just another brutal symptom of Samantha's absence and he wondered how well she was faring - wherever she was.

Schulte renewed his focus to the file in his hand. A possibility immediately leapt from the page he had turned to, causing him to smile.

"Dain," he said quietly - turning around.

The silent giant appeared instantly in front of him and Schulte showed him the page from the file. The man remained as if a statue. Only his eyes moved to the page and then back.

"Follow me to this location. We will go together to retrieve our esteemed professor."

Dain offered only a slight bow of his head as he shimmered in the air before vanishing completely.

Schulte threw back the last of his brandy and set the glass on a nearby table. Adjusting his tie and coat, he smiled. As he shimmered into nothingness, his final word floated through the empty room, "*Excellent*!"

*T*en

Baghdad, Iraq; 2002

The meeting room was a large library. Shelves of books stood in solemn rows, highlighted by elegant sconce lighting. Smug faces greeted Sterling as he stepped into the room. Each had a condescending smirk that further infuriated him. He made a count as he let his gaze fall on each of the occupants of the room. Not counting Duncan, there were four armed guards. Osama Bin Laden sat smiling in a chair towards the center, Saddam Hussein was seated just to his left. Mr. Unknown would make a total of eight.

Sitting behind a huge, Victorian desk and sporting a fifty thousand dollar Westmancott suit, sat Mr. Unknown. Sterling's anger reached new heights when he realized that the mysterious voice belonged to a well known, long standing United States Senator from Illinois and Chairman of the Armed Services, Senator Theodore Godescalcus Schulte.

Sterling's eyes grew wide and he made a rush for the man. He knew before the attempt was made that it was a futile effort, but he needed to force a confrontational defeat. The butt of a rifle stock immediately impacted with the back of Sterling's head and he collapsed to the floor.

Laughter filtered through the room as Sterling was pulled roughly back to his feet. An armed Iraqi guard held him on his left. His former subordinate - Second Lieutenant Lance Duncan - held him on the right.

"Major Jack Sterling," Senator Schulte gloated haughtily as he relaxed back into his chair. "Welcome to our little get together. I was beginning to wonder when you would arrive."

Sterling looked to his right, locking Duncan's eyes to his own.

"Do not blame Lieutenant Duncan for the loss of your team, Major Sterling," Schulte smiled. "He was simply following my orders. The lieutenant will be formally commended for the work he has done here today."

"Good, perhaps that will bring him some peace in the few short minutes he has to live," Sterling replied very quietly - his gaze still locked on Duncan.

More laughter around the room as Duncan swallowed hard.

Sterling's steely gaze found the Senator. "You killed three good Americans. The only reason I would consider allowing you to live is to expose you for the traitorous piece of shit you are!"

A rifle butt impacted hard with the back of Sterling's head again and he dropped to his knees, his arms spread between his two captors. They forced him back to his wobbly feet.

"I think not, Major," Schulte smiled confidently. "It is you that will be blamed for this unfortunate debacle. The political fallout will undoubtedly cause the United States to defer any upcoming Iraqi campaign. The international outrage your actions ignite here today will give us the breathing room we need."

"Breathing room?" Sterling asked in an attempt to remain conscious. His head ached and his knees were on the verge of buckling.

Schulte ignored the question. "Try not to take it personally, Major. I merely needed a lamb that had the talent to get inside this palace. For reasons that will become clear in a few moments, you and your team were the logical choice."

The door suddenly opened and two Republican Guardsmen entered dragging a bloodied figure between them. It was Lieutenant Neal Anderson, badly hurt and nearly unrecognizable from the beating he had just endured. Dropping him roughly to the floor, the two soldiers saluted Saddam and then turned and exited the way they had come.

Duncan and the guard held Sterling from running to his fellow Ranger's aid and he seethed weakly against their grip.

"It appears we have a survivor Major," Schulte said happily as he stood and walked casually over to stand in front of Sterling. "You see, Major. It is not as if I take lightly the supreme sacrifice your men are giving here today. It is merely a necessity. A means to end."

Addressing a ranking guardsman near the door - Schulte commanded, "Captain Rashid, if you would do the honors."

Schulte stared into Sterling's eyes as Captain Rashid pulled a large buoy knife from a sheath. Pulling Anderson's head back by his hair, Rashid slid the razor sharp edge across the helpless Ranger's throat. The skin separated easily as the blade burrowed deep into Anderson's flesh. Anderson's eyes flickered rapidly and his body twitched as blood pumped from the opened artery.

"NO!" Sterling pulled against the iron grip of the men that held him, but gave out quickly from apparent exhaustion.

Schulte smiled casually and turned from Sterling - speaking in Arabic, "My apologies Mr. President for the mess. I am sure that the American government will be happy to provide for a new carpet."

Saddam grinned good-naturedly.

Sterling began to sob in defeat and he let his body droop between his two captors.

As Anderson's thrashing subsided, Schulte turned back to Sterling, "I give your men the dignity of a quick finish, Major."

Rashid stared balefully at Sterling from across the room as he cleaned his knife blade on Anderson's uniform.

Schulte returned to his seat. He said with a detached finality, "You have always been a good soldier, Major. Let's see if your legacy remains intact."

The fight had apparently left Sterling and he sagged further against his captors. He could feel their grip loosen as their arms tired of supporting his weight. Sterling sank his chin to his chest in defeat.

A nod from Schulte and Sergeant Duncan took a step back and pointed his Berretta directly at Sterling's temple. It was the last mistake he would ever make.

Sterling's perceptions heightened, his senses sharpened. A welcome warming sensation inside his chest sprang to life. He could sense the beads of sweat that began to form at the base of Duncan's hairline and the musky smell of his adrenaline as it erupted through his pores - enunciating the turmoil within him. The pull of each muscle as his finger tightened fractionally around the trigger. The resigned look of determination and the anticipated blink of an eye that told Sterling the exact second that his finger would pull that trigger.

Duncan's finger squeezed and Sterling snapped his head backwards at that exact instant. The explosion blew through the room as the subsonic round narrowly missed Sterling's nose. The concussion of the projectile lacerated the side of Sterling's face before slamming deep into the chest of the guard on his left.

His arms now free, Sterling - no longer the beaten captive - raked his boot hard down Duncan's shin, slamming it full force into the top of the inexperienced Ranger's foot. He felt the sickening give of the bone as it yielded to the impact. Duncan screamed in agony as Sterling easily pulled the gun loose from his grip. He twisted swiftly, expertly breaking Duncan's wrist. Slamming the gun butt hard into the lieutenant's nose, Sterling grabbed the startled man's arm and swung him around for use as a human shield.

Captain Rashid was quick with his firearm and was the first to begin firing as he searched for cover behind a bookshelf that lay to his left. The remaining guards were slower, but they found their stride quickly.

A number of rounds from Rashid's pistol pounded into Duncan's chest, propelling him and Sterling backwards. Duncan's vest prevented much of the penetration of the rounds, but the hollow points used by Rashid shattered his ribs with every impact - its fragmenting shrapnel finding exposed flesh.

Duncan's screaming was drowned by the explosive report of gunfire erupting throughout the enclosed room. The guards dove behind bookcases, Saddam and Bin Laden, scrambled for cover. Everyone was searching for shielding from the ricocheting metal fragments.

Except one.

Senator Schulte stood defiantly, staring at Sterling. His gaze not without malevolence, but also stoic. Sterling brought his sights to bear on Schulte and fired several successive rounds but remarkably, the senator stood as before. Sterling again attempted to find him in his sights, but the man seemed to shimmer - the projectiles refusing to find their mark.

Rounds aimed at Sterling from the two inexperienced guards' erratic gunfire, had exploded the window behind Sterling and he had every intention of using it to his advantage.

Taking careful aim next to Duncan's head, Sterling adjusted his breathing. A guard peered around a table, and Sterling fired two rounds into his face. The report of the pistol exploded Duncan's eardrum and he screamed from his newfound pain.

Sterling's fine tuned sensory perception was working his mind through scenarios of escape. He knew Rashid was his most experienced and deadly adversary. The remaining guard was too inexperienced and panicked to be a serious threat. Rashid's magazine was now empty and

Sterling was figuring the man had at least two reserves and would be returning to cover to reload. There was one last unknown variable, and Sterling was instantly rewarded. The door burst open and he immediately cut down the two guards that attempted to come through.

Sterling's magazine was now empty and his mind began to work through avenues of escape. As he anticipated, Rashid had dove for cover to reload giving Sterling very little time. A decision needed to be made - certainly when Rashid had reloaded, he would find his intended target.

Suddenly, the entire library seemed to shimmer - as if the heat of the desert began to bake the room. Time began to slow, the air becoming thick. Sterling could see Rashid coming from cover. He was raising his arm, each step agonizingly slower than the last - and slower still until he finally came to a stop. The room stopped shimmering and an eerie dead pan quiet invaded.

Turning to the only moving thing in the room, Sterling was even more startled to discover Schulte walking toward him. The smile on his face wide. "Please, Major. Won't you join me?"

Eleven

Waset, Kemet - (Thebes, Egypt); c. 1550 BCE

Pen-Nekhbet touched Ipu's fingers to his own with a slight bow of his head, accepting her invitation to converse. "Pen-Nekhbet of Nekheb, royal scribe for his majesty - first in line for Royal herald," he said as modestly as he could manage - yet with enough boastfulness to keep her interest.

The designation of *"First in Line"* would be his and every other courtier's temporary title that evening. It was an honorary designation for those that had advanced with promotion until the formal announcement that would be made during the evening's festivities. The following morning the respective titles would be permanent.

"I am a nurse maiden to the palace nursery, first in line for palace nurse - second class," Ipu replied - her eyes mirroring her smile.

An impressive advancement for one so young. Pen-Nekhbet thought of asking her age, but reconsidered - thinking it a rude question so soon into their conversation. "May I offer you some wine?" He asked instead.

Ipu tilted her head with a sweet accepting smile.

Together, they walked across the room to the banquet table. Downing the last of his wine as they approached, Pen-Nekhbet was reminded of the recent sugary assault on his taste buds and instead, ordered a beer for himself.

Suddenly - from across the room - the mysterious cloaked figure he had seen before reappeared in Pen-Nekhbet's periphery vision. "Do you see that?" He asked Ipu

But by the time she turned to look, the figure was gone. Vanished just as mysteriously as it had before.

Ignoring Ipu's questioning look, Pen-Nekhbet shook his head. Attempting to elude a growing feeling of apprehension, he offered a casual comment, "Never mind. It must have been a figure of imagination."

The two of them found a quiet corner and began to talk easily with each other:

They discussed the meaningful details of their lives and families. Their time spent on palace grounds and at various temples of their patron gods. Loved ones that had come and gone and their hopes and plans for the future. Pen-Nekhbet gradually began to forget the cloaked figure that seemed to be taunting him from a distance.

Suddenly, a great number of horns blasted over the cacophony of the crowd. A near deafening announcement of the arrival of his majesty and living god; King Seqenenre Tao.

Great cheering rose above the ear splitting scream of the horns as the litter - bearing the great King Tao - was lowered to the floor in front of the royal dais and throne. The cheering intensified when his majesty emerged, adorned in a stark white, linen skirting cinched tight around his waist. A ceremonial wolf's tail dangling from the waistline. A single, leather sash was draped fashionably across his chest. Two gold and turquoise bands, held firm around his impressive biceps were complimented by a large, similarly bejeweled necklace that hung low from his shoulders. Atop his head sat the *Hedjet*; the royal crown of Upper Egypt.

A large, covered object was delivered to the dais. With singular flair, the cover was removed revealing the *Sekhemty*; the double crown of unification of the two lands of Egypt - the object of the evenings climatic, albeit somewhat premature finale.

Following on King Tao's heels amidst the ongoing fanfare, heir apparent and current Vizier, Ka-Mose entered the room and took his seat to the right of Tao - followed directly by his younger brother and family namesake, Ah-Mose.

The family name of Ah-Mose had been legendary for several royal generations - Pen-Nekhbet remembered from his studies. From Tao's father - Senakhtenre Ah-Mose - to his father's father and his father before that. Tradition would be upheld that Ka-Mose and Ah-Mose - respectively - were named heirs to the crown.

The unspoken secret that could only be heard amidst hushed whispers throughout the palace was that Ka-Mose and his younger brother Ah-Mose, were almost certainly not blood relation to Tao - despite the family name. Neither brother looked anything like the king; both Ka-Mose and Ah-Mose were tall with shocking blond waves of hair. Whereas Tao had darker hair and was much shorter and stouter. From where the two brothers had therefore originated was a juicy mystery. A salacious morsel of palace intrigue that the courtiers never spoke of outside of their own trusted circles.

Twelve

Baghdad, Iraq; 2002

Puffs of paper, ruined book covers and bits of odd debris hung impossibly suspended - motionless in the stifling air. Rashid - his arm swinging up, his gun searching for its target - was mystically frozen in place as were the Republican guardsmen that had burst through the door - captured in their final act. The bright glow that had once radiated from the wall sconces had degraded into an annoyingly dim pulse as an eerie silence overtook the room.

"Relax Major. Everything will soon return to normal." Schulte, his voice flat - devoid of any resonance in the thick, dead air, indicated to a nearby chair.

Unsure of what was occurring, Sterling chose to stand where he was - keeping Duncan's immobile body between him and Senator Schulte. He kept his empty gun pointed steady at the senator in the hopes that the appearance of the threat would suffice. "What's happening?" Sterling asked - more calmly than even he anticipated.

Schulte smiled, giving his pants a gentle tug as he took a seat. "I have given us a little time together - undisturbed. A moment to get reacquainted - as it were. Please, have a seat." He gestured again to a seat opposite him.

Sterling was still attempting to grasp what was occurring. The impossible imagery seemed too fantastic to accept, yet so familiar as to not. His eyes roved around the room in quasi-disbelief of the immobilization of everyone - save him and Senator Schulte.

"Believe it or not," Schulte said conversationally. "I have spent a great deal of time searching for you. Imagine how pleasantly surprised I was to find that you were now a member of the American military. A Ranger, no less - Major Jack Sterling. Once a soldier always a soldier, I guess." - Schulte smiled in a disarming manner - "I apologize for the theatrics..." - Waving his hand across the room - "...But I had to create a diversion to get you here. Mostly to determine that you were in fact who I thought you were and to share a few memories together. Hopefully undo any negative connotations that may have been created in that sieved mind of yours. Please, have a seat."

Sterling continued to ignore the invitation - his eyes narrowing, "You think this is some kind of goddamned reunion?"

"I had hoped that your memory had improved by now," Schulte continued conversationally - as if the freezing of time was an everyday occurrence. "It is much easier to converse with each other if you could simply come to grips with who you are." Schulte sighed - spreading his hands in resignation and shaking his head, "Ah, but I guess that's the problem with amateurs making life-altering decisions without regard to the consequences - is it not?" He smiled, "The never-ending story of mankind."

"What the hell are you talking about?"

Schulte leaned forward, "I'm talking about the scrambled eggs you have tossing around in your head, Major. You have wasted an enormous amount of time forgetting who you are and it has become increasingly tiresome over the years that we have to keep dancing to this same tune." - A small pause as he leaned back in his seat - "But perhaps that is the cross we both must bear." He cleared his throat as he cocked his head gently to the side - a slight smile forming.

"How are you doing this?" Sterling asked - his gaze level with the Senator as his mind evaluated attack and escape scenarios. "How have you managed to stop time like this?"

Schulte raised his eyebrows, "Oh, I have not stopped time, Major. I am merely casting us backwards in time in repeating intervals. Small milliseconds in rapid succession. We have one foot in two worlds. To those around us, we merely look like we are..." - Searching for a word - "...*Shimmering,*" he said with a bit of a smile.

Sterling appeared confused, as he searched for a memory. This all seemed familiar to him, but only on the outer reaches of his mind. As if he should know what was occurring, but couldn't quite grasp the significance.

"Let me enlighten you, Major. You have felt a growing, familiar tingle in your chest. It warms you. It calls to you. But it also triggers the dreams. Vague, indistinct images that plague you even in your waking hours. Your entire life you have been tormented with visions. Visions of places and people familiar to you, but impossible to know."

Sterling was stunned and his face told that story.

Schulte continued, "Have you ever stopped to consider, that the dreams are significantly more than that?" The heavy silence seemed to become more pronounced as Schulte's smile broadened. "Let me help you remember."

Thirteen

Baghdad, Iraq; 2002

Sterling had heard enough and stood straight. Pulling away from the immobile body of Lieutenant Duncan, he walked toward Schulte with a steely determination. "You're a shit bag traitor. Consorting with the enemy of the American people. You are a disgrace, and today is the day you die."

Schulte was still seated, his legs crossed. Instead of responding to the advancing ranger, he spied a dish of shelled peanuts on the nearby desktop and popped one into his mouth. His nonchalant attitude caused a moment of perplexity for Sterling. The ranger had just informed the Senator that he was set to kill him. Sterling lunged at the Senator with a forearm. The force of which was set to break the senator's neck. But much to his dismay, the Senator had shimmered into nothingness.

Sterling stumbled into the chair that Senator Schulte had just been sitting in - falling to the floor on top of the toppled chair. Quickly coming to his feet, he whirled into the room. Schulte was standing in front of the window, peering down into the swimming pool below. Casually putting a peanut into his mouth. His demeanor was as relaxed as before - as if nothing had transpired.

Schulte tilted his head, his brief laughter subsiding. "You know, it never fails to amaze me that the so-called *new ideas*, and beastly behavior that people engage in, is so often a repeat of old actions with new names."

Sterling began a swift walk towards the senator. He wasn't sure how the man had managed to dodge the vicious attack that had been launched, but he wasn't going to dodge what the ranger now had in mind.

Schulte suddenly put a finger in the air, "Be careful Major. I would hate for a repeat of your last attack to end with a sudden flight out this window. The damage you would sustain would most likely trigger your amnesia again."

Sterling stopped in his tracks, considering - *Amnesia? Again?*

Schulte turned - now facing the Ranger, "Notice how you - yourself - could not understand the failure of your attack. Yet you were set to make the same mistake again. All within the span of a few seconds. A perfect example of the observation I have just made." - He smiled - *"Fascinating."*

Senator Schulte's voice was still flat, lacking vibrancy. He began to walk purposefully around the room. "Somewhere - at sometime - *The Machine* has been activated." - His left hand gestured into the air - "It is pulling on us. Letting us know it is there. It touches each of us that are joined, and we can use it to our own desires." Schulte was suddenly next to Sterling - his eyes focused with intent, "Tell me Major Sterling, what is it that *you* desire?"

Sterling was at a loss. His eyes searched low for an answer that he knew he should have, but only flashes of dreams played across his mind. "Justice," he finally managed to answer - pulling from a distant dream. "I want Justice. Justice for my team, for my country. I want justice from dirt bag politicians like you."

Schulte smiled - his eyes narrowing, *"Excellent.* Tell me Major, what does that justice you espouse look like? What action on your part would bring about the proprietary brand of justice that would satisfy the thirst of blood you possess?"

Sterling did not know how to answer such a loaded question and he was growing weary of the endless drivel the Senator was spewing. He began to focus again on attack and escape scenarios.

Without waiting for an answer, the Senator began to talk. "A very long time ago, I saw the promise of a young man. He was bright and motivated. He also had an unreasonably haughty sense of justice, no doubt spawned and nurtured by his father - also a military man of some standing.

"This young man, as it turned out, was an exceptional warrior. Swift and skilled. But also intelligent. Brilliant in fact. I had decided that I could use such an idealistic young man as my right hand. And - through a series of cleverly designed forays into the political underbelly of that time - I arranged for his advancement."

Schulte now stood over one of the two dead republican guards lying by the door. Leaning down, he grabbed one of their side-arms and checked the chamber. "Through much subterfuge and coercions - as often exist throughout any political world - I brought this soldier through the ranks to sit at my side. But young men are often naïve; unable to grasp a larger picture. He became swayed by the propaganda of my opponent and we fell at odds." - Schulte's voice changed briefly to one of reminiscence - "It was a shame, he would have been part of an unstoppable team."

Schulte stood back up - a smile and slight tilt of his head. "But that is the chaotic nature of life."

Sterling began to breathe heavy as Schulte walked towards him with the pistol. The ranger was effectively unarmed and he began to envision plans of attack. But just as Schulte came within point blank range, the Senator flipped the gun around and handed the weapon to Sterling - butt first.

"I'm offering you another chance, Major. I can give you back your memories. To help you understand who you truly are and give you a chance to bring about that brand of justice you so desire. To right the wrongs of so much of the world's troubles."

"By getting into bed with shit-bags like these," Sterling indicated around the room with the pistol.

Schulte smiled - looking around the room, "These people in this room think their methods are justified to meet their lofty superior goals - as we all do." He tilted his head, "I find it deeply interesting that self-proclaimed pacifists and others that wear their god of so-called peace on their sleeves will insist on you living as they do. So much so that they will blow you up, maim you and destroy your lives and livelihood to ensure you follow the same emotional path as they do." - Gesturing around the room - "What I find even more interesting is that their methods often work."

Sterling narrowed his eyes, "Yet you seem to be in league with them."

Schulte waved his hand dismissively, "They are a tool. A mindless means to an end."

"Is that what I am, senator? A mindless means to an end?"

Schulte shook his head slowly, "No, my boy. You are so much more than that. You are exactly what this world needs. Let me help you remember."

The room suddenly began to shimmer again. Time was beginning to advance - the stillness of the room was shattered.

"Think it over, Major," Schulte said with a smile. "And do be careful when you go out that window. I'd like for you to keep your memory intact as much as possible."

Fourteen

Waset, Kemet - (Thebes, Egypt); c. 1550 BCE

The doors to the chamber burst open - breaking Pen-Nekhbet from his reverie of the previous evening. He turned to the doors just as two royal guards entered, taking positions to either side of the entrance way. Two other guards trailed a daunting figure into the room - breaking from him once inside. Taking positions at either window - offering an effective blockade to all entrance points - they eyed Pen-Nekhbet stoically.

The imposing individual that had been under such intense guard had been named co-regent with Lord Tao at the advancement ceremony of last night's festivities. Ka-Mose's promotion to co-regent with his father, had come with the anticipation of Tao's diplomatic visit north. It allowed for ongoing control of Upper Egypt and protection from the Nubian tribes of *Kusi* while Tao was away from *Waset. "Merely a precautionary measure,"* had been the cautious tone taken at the ceremony.

Ka-Mose was indeed an epitomizing embodiment of a king. His eyes burned black within a stony stare as he regarded Pen-Nekhbet, but softened only slightly as the hint of a smile appeared.

Pen-Nekhbet lowered his eyes in genuflection. He had admittedly been looking forward to this meeting with Ka-Mose. Anxiously. With an anticipation - and a confidence - that the meeting would be beneficial to his career.

Born only eighteen years previous into the family of a career military man named *Baba*, and a freed woman named *Ebana*. Pen-Nekhbet had - to some degree - been expected to follow in his father's footsteps with the great expectation of achieving royal rank. With the destination of palace placement a seemingly foregone conclusion, the family had sacrificed much to pay for Pen-Nekhbet's schooling. Choosing for his son to achieve rank through academia had been his father's idea and his father had died a happy and proud man when his son had been accepted to enter the ranks of the *Royal Scribes*.

The position had served the intellect of Pen-Nekhbet well. Even from an early age, Pen-Nekhbet showed a strong aptitude for reading and writing. He was a born mathematician - possessing an uncanny wisdom of the aged and a strong sense of justice. Throughout his school age years, he was considered a hero to the underdogs. A protector of the weak and a champion of integrity. It also didn't hurt that he was achingly attractive. Tall, with wavy black hair - when he was allowed to let it grow- and ice blue eyes that turned many a lady's head - young or old.

His father had also schooled him in the art of combat and Pen-Nekhbet remained undefeated in his town's warrior class. With his schooling well rounded, the entry level position into the Royal Scribes only seemed to be befitting of his status and abilities. A stepping stone to an even greater career within the palace.

Last night had been the crowning jewel of that great perseverance; having finally been rewarded with the official position of Royal Herald and Seal Bearer. Recording the movements of battle and palace intrigue, while remaining only a breath away from the king at all times.

Ka-Mose spoke first - as was customary, "Greetings, Pen-Nekhbet of Nekheb - son of Ebana. I hope your needs and your desires remain few and fulfilled. May the temple of Ah-Mun look favorably upon you and yours."

"Yours, your majesty," Pen Nekhbet returned, increasing his bow - grateful for the blessing. "May Ah-Mun also look favorably upon the house of Ah-Mose, my lord."

Ka-Mose got directly to the point.

"Congratulations are in order - for both of us. Your elevation to membership of the house of Ah-Mose as its Herald *and* Bearer of the King's Seal is impressive - the position to be held in great reverence."

"Yes, my lord," Pen-Nekhbet replied - the weight of the King's Seal around his neck seemingly more pronounced. He was reminded that Ka-Mose had been instrumental in the achievement of his current rank and he felt an eerie, yet familiar feeling run through him. An unshakable idea that Ka-Mose had an underlying, ulterior motive. It seemed rather convenient that his own fortunate set of circumstances arising from Hornakht's death and his rapid rise to such a coveted position, had been so... seamless.

Almost, - dare he say, - orchestrated?

But what ulterior motives would Ka-Mose have in mind?

He remembered having this same odd feeling during the political debates of the previous evening's festival. Ipu had not been allowed to attend the closed door session, but Pen-Nekhbet's new position dictated his attendance:

Lord Tao sat distant, above the fray; listening; judging - as Ka-Mose, Ah-Mose, and a handful of high level advisors hashed out details of Tao's ambassadorial visit north - to Lower Egypt and the land of the Asiatic - and the anticipated repercussions of his meeting with the northern prince, *Apophi*.

The first to speak was High Steward for the palace, *Imhotep*, "We need not be rash in our stance, my lord. You now wear the crown of unification and it will soon be sanctified. For too many years we have been in a struggle with the Asiatic. Yet, finally - under your keen leadership - Egypt is at peace. And that peace should not be squandered. All of Egypt are loyal to you as far north as *Qis*. As far south as *Elephantine*, all are strong and dedicated. Egypt is at peace and our people are happy. Our land is fruitful and our cattle are safe. We have little want." - Imhotep opened his hands wide in gesture - "The Asiatic trade freely their grain to feed our people and our livestock.

"To sacrifice our prosperity out of spite against the Asiatic - when we are so close to sanctifying peace for generations to come - is foolhardy. The people are tired of war. If Apophi promises to keep taxes low and the toll roads trouble free for safe passage through the *Retjenu...*" he said - referring to the lands and the people of Kanan; the area east of Egypt surrounding the Great Green Sea borders - "...all of us may share in many splendid years of prosperity. Our people can well afford Asiatic tariffs - they are too insignificant to go to war over. Apophi may hold the Lower region of Egypt, but you - my lord - are now king of *all* of Egypt."

Uneasy murmuring floated through the room as Imhotep confidently settled back in his chair. Silence eventually settled through the chamber as all eyes and ears came to rest on the vizier and newly crowned co-regent.

Ka-Mose tilted his head to compliment a condescending smile he wore. He pompously chuckled with a slight shake of his head. Slowly - as if he now had to address children in a school room - he stood.

"My dear, Imhotep," Ka-Mose began through a heavy sigh. "I struggle at times to find the answer as to how a fool such as you can be allowed to sweep the palace floors, much less hold any ranking position in its court."

Stifled laughter bounced through the chamber halls. Imhotep lifted his chin in defiance to Ka-Mose's belittling, but remained silent.

Ka-Mose continued, "I should like to know what serves the strength of our king, our people and our land that a prince in Avaris - and another in Kusi - remains united in defiance to Egypt and its people? Each retaining their own slice of *our* land. And to this day, we continue to acquiesce to their ongoing demands.

"When the justified king, Amenemhat built the canals of *Mer-Wer*, he was kind enough to put these lowly Kanan, *Habiru* to work..."

Uneasy murmuring interrupted Ka-Mose's speech; a mild rebuke at his use of slang. *Habiru* was a taboo word meaning an unclean person. A disparaging epithet that referred to the nomads of the Retjenu - the land of the Kanan people along the coastlands of the Great Green Sea. The *Habiru* were known as thieves, slaves, and unskilled laborers. Untrustworthy mercenaries and rebels that plagued the entire lands of the Kanan.

"I speak the truth," Ka-Mose insisted. "We all know that our euphemistic term referring to them as *Asiatic* is further acquiescence to *their* demands. A title they do not deserve. They themselves were forced from their land by their own brethren. They are the lowest among even their own kind. Even our Kanan brothers throughout the Retjenu call these invaders of Egypt, *Habiru* - yet somehow *we* are held in contempt for referring to them in kind?

"I will ask this court again - why must we continue to bow to their demands? Hear me, Egypt. Shall we continue to couch our words in rhetoric more pleasing to Egypt's oppressor, so as to satisfy some ill-defined, delicate sensibility of our cowardly brethren? I say, *no more*."

Ka-Mose's passion was awakening and it was becoming contagious.

"We are Egyptians!"

He cast his gaze around the room, "When our great king, Amenemhat graciously gave these *Habiru* work at the Mer-Wer canals, they repaid his generosity with invasion. A soft invasion to be sure, but an invasion nonetheless. Amenemhat gave them land to work with their promise they would return to their own homes at the end of the harvest season. They were to retreat to their own villages throughout the Retjenu. Instead these invaders brought with them their families. Entire tribes of *Habiru* pushed our people south. They took our lands with their settlement and their incessant demands. Their temples replaced our own. They took over our homes and our Necropolis'. We have even given them sovereignty over *our* greatest monuments. To the point that to this day, generations of our own people have no conception of their own history.

"Make no mistake my lord, we our losing our culture, our history and our way of life. Even now our people continue to be forced south. And with the *Habiru's* ally in Kusi pushing on our southern border, Egypt stands at the brink of extinction. There is destined to arrive a time when the *Habiru* shall tire of our existence. We must understand that co-existence is *always* an exercise in futility!

"They *will* force us from our homes. They *will* slaughter our people in the streets. They *will* make it a crime to be Egyptian and then what shall we do? Stand proudly on our laurels and principles? Take pride in the fact that *we* were the kinder, gentler people as our throats are sliced in the night?"

Heavy murmurs erupted throughout the hall. Emotions were running high as Ka-Mose spoke and Pen-Nekhbet could feel the passion thickening.

Ka-Mose persisted, "*If* they keep their taxes low," he said contemptuously. "And *if* they keep the roads to Retjenu safe. And, *if* I were a god I could direct the sun.

"You offer nothing more but ongoing acquiescence, Imhotep. This is *our* land that they are taxing *our* people for, to their own pleasure. It matters little that our people can afford it; *our property is not theirs to take!*"

More cheering erupted through the hall as everybody's passion was now brimming.

"None of us can travel through our own land, from Waset to Mennefer, where we are not accosted by the *Habiru*. None can find peace or justice with the claustrophobic taxation imposed by these *Asiatic*," He spoke the last word with contempt.

"It is the epitome of arrogance on their part to demand tribute, and Egypt's own stupidity and timidity to allow it. When will Egypt have enough and finally stand up to this ongoing invasion?

"When Egypt's back lies broken from having stretched to its end, is that when our people will finally have enough? Then only to realize - too late - we no longer have a back with which to stand?

"No, my fellow Egyptians - *'no more'*. Even now, we treat our majesty's crowning of Egyptian unification as a gift given by these *Habiru* - when it should never have been relinquished in the first place! Lord Tao's crowning of unification of the two lands is Egypt's birthright. It should no longer be considered Asiatic land to which our people are taxed at the pleasure of invaders. It is now Egyptian land that we are reclaiming for our own. That is the message this meeting with prince Apophi should clearly define!"

The response from the crowd was thunderous. Applause resounded throughout the hall. People stomped their feet and shouted with unbridled excitement.

Finally Tao silently raised his hand to quiet them.

Imhotep jumped from his seat, "Is it war you insist on putting our people through?" He shouted hoarsely at Ka-Mose, "War is now what you propose to declare, for I find no reasonable interpretation of your words otherwise! And neither shall Apophi!" Imhotep was furious at being upstaged and continued to rant, "Your rhetoric will lead to the slaughter of the women and children of the Asiatic - and of Egypt! Our people can well afford the tribute Apophi demands..."

And, so it continued.

Ka-Mose and the rest of the court listened quietly as Imhotep metaphorically produced his own length of rope and began to tie his own noose. Everyone could see the leaps of illogic and defeatism that he was espousing.

Pen-Nekhbet then saw Ka-Mose's eyes meet Ah-Mose. The brothers shared a knowing, silent stare for just a moment.

Then, Ka-Mose's gaze found Pen-Nekhbet and a small smile flashed across his face.

And - it was at that moment that Pen-Nekhbet stared into the face of Ka-Mose - that he realized that war was not his end game. That there was something else entirely on Ka-Mose's mind.

An ulterior motive.

But, what was it?

What was Ka-Mose's plan?

Fifteen

Brooklyn, New York; c. 1970's

The crowd outside the café had swelled. Hal pulled young Larimer Lownsbury from his fallen mother's side and held him close. The boys anguish was contagious and Hal was quickly moved to his own tears. The grief was replaced with trepidation though when his attention was caught by a familiar face. A sharp-dressed man stood on the other side of the street - unmoving. His aura was menacing - nearly visible with animosity as he watched the chaos that was occurring.

Hal locked eyes with the man, his stare was cautiously daring. But the only response from the man was a slight ominous smile accompanied by a subtle cock of the head. The two remained locked in this stare-down until the stranger gave a single nod of his head and vanished into thin air.

The crowd had circled around Lownsbury's mother. One of the firemen was checking for a pulse. Another began yelling for medical help.

Hal stared impassively across the street until he was certain the man would not be returning, and then focused his attention to the alley into which Professor Lownsbury had stumbled.

Senator Theodore Godescalcus Schulte could not have been more pleased.

The otherwise quiet Brooklyn street that he and Dain had materialized on, was alive with activity in spite of the late hour. Something had happened to a nearby establishment, but as to the particulars; Schulte couldn't have cared less.

Nor did Schulte have any regard as to the disposition of a young, grief stricken boy that wept inconsolably over the prone body of a woman that lay on a sidewalk across the street. And he offered only a mild consideration to the throng of people that had gathered to witness all the misery that life had chosen to dish up at this unfortunate hour.

Schulte's pleasure emerged when his eyes came to rest on a transient that had wondered into the bedlam surrounding a deceased young woman. Although the man was disheveled and filthy with acres of tangled growth, there was no mistaking the lanky build. The way he carried himself as he navigated towards the nearby side alley. His clothes - torn and tattered - were still instantly recognizable.

Professor Larimer Lownsbury.

This had turned out to be easier than he thought.

Dain had been standing next to Schulte. His body - still and silent - enveloped in the shadow of the nearby building. A dark silhouette that unnervingly blended into his surroundings, Schulte could barely discern his essence from even a few feet.

Schulte gestured, pointing to the scruffy professor who was staggering into the dark alley. Dain offered a slight tilt of his head as he shimmered into vapor.

It would only be a few moments now. Dain would deliver the good professor to the mountain retreat, Schulte would meet them there and he and the professor would have a few laughs and reminisce as they chatted over the whereabouts of Samantha.

Schulte sighed - smugly. He glanced back over to the commotion gathering on the intersection. Fire crews and camera trucks were splayed dramatically through the street; blocking traffic and creating a singular turmoil themselves. His eyes locked with a Samaritan that had stopped to help the grief stricken boy and was - even now - consoling the youngster. It was a familiar face. A face Schulte knew very well, in fact. It was a face that stretched back through generations and ages. A face that had bewitched him for centuries.

There was only one reason why the man was here.

Schulte could see no reason for remaining any longer; he would choose to wait for Dain and the professor in the comfort of his mountain home. With a slight incline of his head to the Samaritan, Schulte vanished into his time stream.

Dain flickered into existence directly behind Professor Larimer Lownsbury - just inside the alley. But as the Dark Man reached out from the shadows of time to seize the man, he disappeared.

Dain stood there for a second, astonished. This was not something he had expected. Lownsbury was a time traveler. That meant he would have to follow the professor's stream to his destination and collect him there.

As Dain prepared to enter his time stream to correct his mistake, something else occurred that instantly dropped the dark giant to his knees.

A man suddenly appeared in front of him.

But this was not just any man. Large in his own right, the newcomer was still dwarfed by Dain's massive bulk. But it made little difference. The newcomer laid a hand on Dain's shoulder and the Dark Man fell to a knee. His head bowed in genuflection.

"Not this one Dain," Hal said gently.

Speaking for the first time in centuries, Dain's voice boomed through the narrow alley - deep and solemn - his echo resonated between the buildings, *"Yes, my lord!"*

Sixteen

Baghdad, Iraq; 2002

Duncan suddenly became dead weight as time resumed its natural cadence. The impact from Rashid's rounds had nearly crushed the lieutenant's chest and had sliced his face to ribbons. His right ear was bleeding, his wrist and nose were broken and he kept drifting in and out of consciousness.

Sterling recovered from the odd time displacement and taking aim with the gun Schulte had handed him, fired two more rounds at Rashid. As Rashid ducked his head back for cover, Sterling spun Duncan around so that the lieutenant's back was to the window. Face to face with the dying soldier, Sterling spat, *"Reap the whirlwind you son of a bitch!"*

Slamming him through the remains of the shattered window, Sterling rode the broken soldier's body from the third story. Duncan's body impacted with a bone crushing thump into the concrete below. The weight of Sterling's impact on top of Duncan's body caused a sickening evacuation of much of his bodily fluids and allowed Sterling's own collision with the concrete to be greatly reduced. He bounced off of the dead body and somersaulted into the swimming pool.

Most of the girls that had been swimming were scrambling to the pool edge to escape the horror that had suddenly erupted around them. Gunfire exploded from the open window above as Rashid began firing into the water. Two of the slower girls became casualties from the hail of bullets - their screams abruptly silenced.

Sterling surfaced at the far side of the pool as Rashid again changed magazines. He climbed from the pool and set off at a dead run for the orange grove and the river beyond. The sounds of pursuit and gunfire were coming from every direction as Sterling ran. He suddenly felt a sharp impact into his left side.

He was hit!

He staggered.

Another impact into his shoulder and yet another found the mid portion of his back. Refusing to let it slow him down, Sterling screamed his determination - diving headfirst into the warm, shallow water of the Tigris River.

The night was alive with explosions as thousands of rounds from dozens of rifles blasted into the water of the Tigris. When the smoke cleared and silence again dominated the Baghdad evening, a brief search of the river's edge revealed nothing.

Major Jack Sterling was gone.

Seventeen

Waset, Kemet - (Thebes, Egypt); c. 1550 BCE

Ulterior motive.

Ka-Mose's voice brought Pen-Nekhbet from his memory, "How do you view your new role as royal official?" Ka-Mose asked again.

"I serve my lord in his desire to bring justice to the people of Egypt," Pen-Nekhbet answered quickly - realizing that Ka-Mose had to ask the question twice.

Ka-Mose's eyebrows raised questionably, "Really? And what is justice, Pen-Nekhbet?"

"Justice is the measure by which fair practice and moral bearing can be sanctified - surely."

Ka-Mose nodded in thoughtful reflection before asking, "So, should an innocent man be punished?"

"Neither should a guilty man go unpunished."

"Should a man who is caught stealing bread to feed his starving family be considered guilty of a sin?"

Pen-Nekhbet paused in thought for just a moment, "I would ask - should the theft of any person's property, by any other person or power - even done so in the name of charity - be justified? Charity is voluntary by its definition. And charity, properly taught to the citizens is how that man could - and should - temporarily feed his own. If a man's need arise - and if he is unable to *temporarily* do so by his own measure - charity is the answer. Theft by his own hand - or theft by a governing agency on his behalf - is theft nonetheless. Theft is not charity, for theft is done so at the expense of another - under duress or force. And theft done so, especially in the false name of charity should be punished accordingly."

Ka-Mose nodded thoughtfully, "And the taking of the land back from the Asiatic. A land they have come to know and love, is that justice for them?"

Pen-Nekhbet was beginning to see where this was going; Ka-Mose was vying for a political ally. Pen-Nekhbet's rapid advancement to Herald and Seal Bearer had been done so with Ka-Mose's endorsement - and he was now being gently reminded of that fact. Ka-Mose was a far more advanced political player and Pen-Nekhbet knew that he needed to tread carefully.

Finally - he gave Ka-Mose a political answer. Not fully committing, but entertaining him with what he thought he might want to hear.

"The Asiatic occupy Egyptian soil, my lord. Is it not justice to the owners of property to be redeemed for their loss? I might ask; where is the justice to the Egyptian people? Egypt is my first concern as an Egyptian and as a servant to my king."

"If it is as Imhotep says…" - Ka-Mose countered - "…That we are destined to slaughter the innocent among the Asiatic, then would the taking of those lives be justified?"

Pen-Nekhbet was momentarily silent, his eyes cast down in thought. *Ulterior Motive.*

"Imhotep did not say *innocent*," Pen-Nekhbet clarified. "He said, *women and children.* There is a distinction."

Ka-Mose smiled - cocking his head, "There are those that would say there is little difference."

There was a long pause as the conversation was digested. Finally Ka-Mose asked, "Tell me, Pen-Nekhbet - what if that which is justified for Egypt, contradicts justice that should be considered for the sake of basic humanity?"

Pen-Nekhbet thought for a long second before replying, "Laying down in pacification should not be done anytime someone wishes to possess that which does not belong to them. That is not any definition of justice. Sometimes, the mere act of survival overshadows any other rationale."

Ka-Mose smiled, "So, the wholesale act of slaughter at times, may be justified - is that what I am hearing you say?"

Pen-Nekhbet blinked.

Ka-Mose quickly rephrased his question, "Tell me what you think, Pen-Nekhbet. Do you think we should bow to the demands of the Asiatic even further, or destroy them. Which option best serves the justice of the Egyptian people?"

Pen-Nekhbet finally answered, "I no longer know the answer, my lord." His hangover was showing little signs of weakening and Ka-Mose's line of questioning was making it worse. Perhaps that was intentional on Ka-Mose's part.

Ka-Mose smiled, "Relax, Pen-Nekhbet of Nekheb. I am merely testing your integrity. There is no wrong or right answer, there is only best judgment based on your individual character. Your character indicates a personal bend towards your own people - as it should. There is no harm in basing the answer to moral dilemmas on what is best for the Egyptian people - *Your people,*" he said again.

Ka-Mose sat silent for a beat before continuing, "I have always believed that it is a short-sided leadership that confuses a citizen - or even a soldier - into equivocating the killing of a woman or child in order to save his own people as somehow wrong. For it is not. That type of dilemma only serves to destroy a person's psyche."

A quizzical look crossed Pen-Nekhbet's face as he contemplated Ka-Mose's words.

Ka-Mose watched him for a long moment before changing the subject, "What do you think of Lord Tao's philosophical stance with the Asiatic?"

Pen-Nekhbet knew that King Tao believed - as Imhotep - that by acquiescence and diplomacy, he could plow sympathy from both peoples; the Asiatic and the Egyptians. It was easy to assume the true purpose of Tao's advancement of Ka-Mose to vizier and co-regent. It was convenient to have a scapegoat to pin war on, if diplomacy were to fail.

"My lord's diplomacy shall be his will."

"I do not want a political answer Pen-Nekhbet, I want your truth," Ka-Mose said roughly.

Pen-Nekhbet was becoming nervous, this line of conversation could lead him into the arena of potential sedition and he had yet to even carry out the first of his duties in his office.

Was this a further test?

Finally, he managed to come up with another political answer, "Lord Tao's first desire is to wear the *Sekhemty*. He is aware - as we all are -

that war is costly and destructive. But I personally have never known acquiescence to lead to lasting peace with anyone."

There was a pause for just a beat and then Pen-Nekhbet clarified, "But I will never go against my king."

Ka-Mose smiled, "I am now second in line to the throne and remain merely a heartbeat away from kingship."

Pen-Nekhbet was nervous, "I do not believe it proper to talk of such things, my lord. His majesty forever lives," he said - indicating that lord Seqenenre Tao was alive.

"Nobody lives forever Pen-Nekhbet," Ka-Mose said with a smile. "Good thing too, wouldn't you say?"

Nobody lives forever.

Pen-Nekhbet noticed that the way Ka-Mose had said those words had been telling. But the subtleness of his inflection was overshadowed by the seditiousness of his line of questioning. Pen-Nekhbet tried in vain to hide his nervousness over the potentially damning implications.

"Relax Pen-Nekhbet, our conversation shall remain private," Ka-Mose said reassuringly. "I will not hold your opinions against you. I encourage them as a matter of fact. It is evident that you will remain loyal to your king, but there is nothing wrong with maintaining your own opinion. As you continue to rise in rank, I shall look forward to your counsel."

Ulterior motive was now a pervasive, ubiquitous thought that Pen-Nekhbet was finding increasingly difficult to ignore.

Eighteen

Mansfield, Connecticut; Modern Day

Getting cleaned up was Lownsbury's prime concern as he scanned the parking lot of the upscale Berkshire condominium unit near Mansfield, Connecticut. It was close to midnight but the small New England town still catered to the innocuous visitor or casual stroller that inhabited most developments. His senses were on full alert for anything that seemed unbefitting; an out of place vehicle or a suspicious loiterer.

The parking lot was clear.

Lownsbury's idea wasn't a great one - he could admit that to himself. But it seemed like the best one he could come up with at the time. After he cleaned up, he could then figure out a place in time to go. Here he had clothes, money and more than anything - if he could get into his condo unnoticed - privacy.

Getting in unnoticed was the trick.

He really had no fear of meeting himself. If his calculations were correct - which they usually were - his current self - under the guise of an east coast lecture tour - had just left for Colorado to begin work on *The Machine* for Senator Schulte. To get into his condo unnoticed, he merely had to make it by Mrs. Brown's window.

Good old Mrs. Brown - Berkshires resident gossip and busybody. Weighing less than the average cocker spaniel and with hair to match, she was a lean, mean, chatting machine. She reminded Lownsbury of

Gladys Kravitz from the old Bewitched television show. Even at this late hour, Mrs. Brown was sure to be awake - making it her business to know what was happening in her little piece of the world.

Somewhere in the distance a dog began to bark. Elsewhere, the distant boom of a car stereo could be heard drawing near - the sound peaking before fading into nothingness. Sounds of life that somehow made Lownsbury feel that much more alone.

Lownsbury breathed deep - a long, low breath - thinking of their recent activities in Colorado. He remembered how Theodore Godescalcus Schulte - a senator from Illinois - had enlisted the help from William Masters, Captain Jack Sterling and himself, to repair and activate a Nazi Time Machine that had been found in the Colorado Rocky Mountains. It had later been discovered by the team that Schulte was already an active time traveler and had been enabling and helping Adolph Hitler in his Socialistic takeover of the world. Playing puppet master to him as well as other deadly dictators throughout history - his sights appeared to have settled on the United States. But having had time to think during his incarceration in seventeenth century Salem Village, Lownsbury was now having doubts that any of them even knew what Schulte's ultimate goals really were.

Salem.

Trapped in time and jailed in Salem Village, Massachusetts for witchcraft, he and Samantha had unwittingly sparked the iconic political tragedy that befell New England in 1692. Lownsbury had barely managed to escape back to his own time, leaving the evil senator's beautiful daughter to her fate. It had been a decision that now made it imperative that Lownsbury never risk being caught by Senator Schulte. Being found by the senator could result in the information of Samantha's whereabouts being extracted and that was a risk they could not afford.

The rest of his team - Captain Jack Sterling and Will Masters - were entrusting him not to return to his former life while they continued the mission to stop the senator from his take-over of the United States. Getting Samantha out of the picture was a tremendous victory in their efforts. A triumph that could not be undone. Lownsbury was determined not to let them down.

But that gnawing feeling that they were continuing to underestimate Schulte persisted.

Lownsbury looked around the parking lot one last time. He knew he could not loiter much longer without drawing unwanted attention to himself. Although he supposed that even if he were seen, it would not be as major a *faux pas* as the one that he had just performed: Taking his team to the strip club in which his mother had worked when he was a young boy and then to the café on the night she died, was not the brightest move that could be made. If that hadn't been a monumental screw up, he didn't know what was.

A quick in and out of his own place for a shower and a change of clothes - he thought - and that would be the end of it.

The parking lot lights were bright and Lownsbury did his best to stay to the shadows as he quickly made his way to the second story landing that led to his condo door. Mrs. Brown's lights were on. It was a certainty she was home and Lownsbury held his breath as he quietly slid past her doorway; stopping just long enough to retrieve his spare key from beneath a loose brick on the large window sill adjacent to his door. Lownsbury quietly slid the key into the lock and slipped inside. Once inside, he silently closed the door and put his back to it - listening - consciously trying to slow his heartbeat that he was almost certain Mrs. Brown could hear. The apartment was quiet. Mrs. Brown's door remained closed and Lownsbury began to relax a little.

Resisting the urge to turn on lights, Lownsbury made his way through the living room and into the kitchen. Retrieving a garbage bag from under the sink, he quickly navigated down the familiar hallway and into the master bathroom. His bathroom had no window, so Lownsbury turned on the lights. Stepping into the shower stall, he retrieved a bottle of medicinal shampoo and a set of hair clippers that he had purchased from a local pharmacy from his bedraggled suit coat. He quickly undressed, pushing the clothes deep into the plastic garbage bag. Plugging the clippers into the bathroom receptacle, he began to methodically shave all the hair from his face and head. He remained inside the shower stall in an effort to control the mess and the lice, and proceeded to get as close to the scalp as the clippers would allow. He put as much of the loose hair as he could inside the plastic bag and tied it shut.

He followed the directions on the bottle of shampoo and within a few minutes, Lownsbury was finally enjoying the first shower he had had in months. He set the water as hot as he could stand it and let the water pour freely over his head and back. He could feel the months of grime sloughing from his body. The hot water warmed his core - the heat finally overtaking the months of cold he had so recently endured.

Standing there as the water pounded against his skin, Lownsbury suddenly felt the full impact of all that he had been through:

From meeting Schulte's sidekick - Gabriel Martinelli - to his stay in Salem's dungeon, to witnessing once again his mother's passing - the effect of all that had transpired fell full-force on Lownsbury's shoulders. Weeping, Lownsbury dropped to his knees in the bottom of the shower. The hot water cascaded over him, washing his burdened body clean.

Nineteen

Baghdad, Iraq; 2002

Doctor Jasmin Al-Bayati stared out of the Omar Bin Yasir Street hospital window and into the night sky. It was the second evening of constant helicopter sweeps and Republican guard searches. Soldiers had been in and out of the hospital for close to twenty four hours now. Their constant searching, interrogations and overall menacing presence, made it difficult for the hospital staff to perform their duties and invoked terror in most of the helpless patients. Many of which had already been victims at the hands of Saddam's regime.

Jasmin folded her stethoscope and deposited it into the large pocket of her smock.

She rubbed her eyes

It was turning into a very long night.

The omnipresence of Baghdad's military necessarily meant that something had happened at the palace the previous evening. But the public could only guess as to the nature of the emergency. Panic among the citizenry had been heightened by the military force searching the streets and that translated into a very busy time for the hospital. But Jasmin's shift was finally coming to an end. She was looking forward to a long hot bath and had been counting the minutes until her shift would be over.

She wrote a notation in the chart of a sleeping patient and placed the clipboard back into the plastic sleeve at the foot of his bed. Most of the patients had been sedated to prevent widespread panic and the quietness of the room was a welcome relief to the chaos of the past several hours. She stopped at the sink and refilled the patient's water pitcher and regarded the weary face in the mirror above the sink that stared back at her.

Jasmin Al-Bayati had always been beautiful. Her long, black hair accentuated penetrating coal black eyes. She had won several beauty contests in her youth - when such contests had been allowed - but her once perfect skin was now showing the tell-tale signs of weariness and sadness. Dark circles underscored her eyes. Eye's now troubled by tragedy that encapsulated her beloved country of Iraq. Tragedy that seemed to grow exponentially every day.

She mumbled a quick prayer for her parents. Gone now at the hands of Saddam's oldest son. A needless heartbreak that still tore at Jasmin's soul and probably would for the rest of her life. A tear rolled down her cheek and she brushed it away as she pulled her eyes from the mirror.

Her shift was over. She could find her solace again in the peaceful confines of her own apartment. She placed the water pitcher on the bedside table and mumbled another quick prayer that there would be no emergency's between here and the hospital exit.

Twenty

Waset, Kemet - (Thebes, Egypt); c. 1550 BCE

Ka-Mose snapped his fingers and Pen-Nekhbet became instantly alert. Fearful that his lingering hangover had caused his concentration to wane and the crown prince had perhaps noticed.

Suddenly, a Kanan slave appeared from nowhere with a wine vessel. Pen-Nekhbet breathed a silent sigh of relief.

Laying two copper mugs on the table between them, the servant poured a healthy helping into both mugs before disappearing as quickly as he appeared.

Taking a large gulp from his mug, Ka-Mose breathed deep with closed eyes - savoring the sugary remains of the alcohol that swam through his sinuses. Finally - he spoke, "More than three hundred years ago - when the *Habiru* poured across our Eastern border - we chose a policy of complacency over brutality because of our reluctance to harm their women and children. So they came - and they came. For years and years they flooded into Egypt. Women and children, with their young men filtered among them. And we did nothing to stop them." - A moment's pause - "This sympathetic viewpoint is where Imhotep's coalition has gathered its strength. He is now prisoner to that position. A position that has allowed the *Habiru* to kill us with our own kind-heartedness. And one that Egypt - unfortunately - may never be able to overcome."

Another breath. Another gulp of wine.

Pen-Nekhbet sipped his wine slowly. His head swimming as a reminder of last night's festivities.

"It wasn't just king Amenenhap's generosity that was the singular motivation for the invasion of Egypt by the *Habiru*, however," Ka-Mose continued. "The truth was the *Habiru* were being pushed out of the Retjenu by the Amurru and other tribes of the Kanan people. They were as unwanted a people to the rest of the Kanan as they have been to the Egyptians. It is simply *our* generosity that allowed them to stay and to thrive."

Ka-Mose leaned closer, "The *Habiru* are a leech, clinging to the teat of Egypt. They will always be as a leech; sucking the life blood of all our people. And now - with Apophi's new demands - they have worn their welcome. You said it best Pen-Nekhbet - it should now be the Egyptian people to whom we owe our allegiance."

And there it was. Pen-Nekhbet's own words now on the table. He realized he had inadvertently played perfectly into Ka-Mose's plans.

Ulterior Motive.

"Tao desires a peaceful unification," Ka-Mose said through a steely, wine-laced breath. "But that is naive fantasy. As you said, his desire is the *Sekhemty*. But appeasement to the *Habiru* has only proven us weak to the rest of the world. That we are a people that can be taken advantage of - either by the Nubians to our south, or the Amurru along our eastern frontier. Both Tao and Imhotep are deeply mistaken of Apophi's motivations - their egos unwilling to cede to any depth of reason."

Ka-Mose brought another taste of wine to his lips. Turning to Pen-Nekhbet, "So perhaps Imhotep is correct; we have two choices. Peace or war. Submission or rebellion. Unfortunately, war may likely be our only salvation."

"Imhotep is also correct in stating that Egypt is weary of war," Pen-Nekhbet replied.

Ka-Mose offered a small chuckle, "War is the nature of man, Pen-Nekhbet." Ka-Mose eyes flashed as he smiled. And then, he leaned close, "You know, there is a second option."

Pen-Nekhbet remained quiet. Not knowing where Ka-Mose was heading.

"What would you say if the *Habiru wanted* to leave Egypt?"

Pen-Nekhbet offered a slight tilt of head, "We are the most prosperous empire in the world. Every Kanan wants to come to Egypt. Especially the *Habiru*. Why would they *want* to leave?"

Ka-Mose leaned back in his chair. A heavy, contented sigh escaping him. Pen-Nekhbet had been hooked with the asking of the question.

"I have had several meetings with my brother - Prince Ah-Mose. Even as Tao prepares to set sail with the sun, my brother and I have put into motion a plan that will work to the benefit of both sides of this perpetual conflict."

Pen-Nekhbet was becoming increasingly nervous the more he listened. He was fully aware of the following morning's agenda. He was preparing to set sail with his majesty at first light - for their journey north and Seqenenre Tao's meeting with Apophi. But he now had knowledge of a scheme that seemed to be in the process of being hatched. As the royal herald, Pen-Nekhbet was *the* chief scribe - privy to all information concerning his majesty's movements and dictates. He was duty bound to reveal his knowledge of possible sedition by the vizier to his majesty.

"Fear not, Pen-Nekhbet," Ka-Mose said - as if reading his mind. "Tao is in full knowledge of our meetings. But we must maintain discretion. Tao must remain on his course of appeasement with Apophi to pacify Imhotep's coalition. Despite his destiny of failure to diplomatically unite both lands."

"We?" Pen-Nekhbet managed.

Ka-Mose smiled, "Apophi agrees that the riches of the Retjenu are an attractive enticement. He has always desired the control of the Retjenu and the powerful trade routes that run through all of the *Djahy*." He said, meaning the whole coastal region of the Retjenu. "Not just *that* trade that flows into Egypt." - A pause - "He has just lacked the muscle to acquire it."

Ka-Mose continued, "Instead of sending our armies to remove Apophi and his people from our cities and monuments, we shall agree to join with him in a campaign into the Retjenu. With our taking of the Retjenu - and the placement of Apophi as the new *Hyksos* of the Kanan people - we would have total control from the Reed Sea to the Hatti in Anatolia. We would control the Retjenu and the entire eastern shores of the Great Green and all areas to the western shore of Sea of the Dead."

Pen-Nekhbet gasped, "Tao has agreed to this? You have negotiated foreign policy behind his back?"

Ka-Mose chuckled into his now empty mug, "Even if Tao's dream of success in his negotiations with Apophi were to be realized, the peace would be fleeting. Tao understands this. But he also understands that Imhotep has powerful allies in his anti-war movement. Tao's meeting must take place as political maneuvering to appease Imhotep's coalition."

There was a long pause. Then Ka-Mose said, "*I* am Lord Tao's contingency plan."

Twenty One

Schulte's Retreat;

Date: Unknown

Schulte anxiously awaited Dain's arrival in the living room of his mountain retreat. His plans had not been going well as of late and this was the first potential for success that he had had since bringing Sterling, Masters and Lownsbury into his fold.

He rubbed his head in angst as he paced.

Perhaps he was merely experiencing mental fatigue brought on as a result of Samantha's absence.

Perhaps

He poured himself a drink. This was more than he usually downed in a day and something inside him told him to stop. Managing to reach an inner compromise, he decided to pace himself instead - mildly sipping the expensive spirits.

His patience waned - *Where was Dain with the professor?*

'Try to be calm,' he told himself. Dain would be along momentarily. The big man had been a faithful servant for so many years, it was hard to imagine anything less than success from him.

Patience.

A mysterious man of magic and the last survivor of a race having long since perished - Dain was as loyal as he was eternal. Archaic - even at the time of Schulte's father's kingdom - Dain lived to serve the royal family of Alysia until the end of time.

His father's kingdom.

The kingdom of Alysia had once been a powerhouse of the known world and was the initial home of the fantastic Orb known as *The Eye of Ra*!

The Orb - in tandem with the Artifact: The Bracelet of Ra - had once given electricity to other kingdoms around the globe and had raised mankind to a level of achievement unrivaled until the modern time. Unbelievingly, his father had squandered the power of the Orb - taking stands against everything Schulte believed. His father could have conquered the world with the power at his fingertips, but he chose instead to follow a different philosophy.

A fool's choice, as far as Schulte was concerned.

He spat.

If his father had only listened to *him* instead of his worthless brother, the kingdom of Alysia would still be in existence and Schulte would have taken his rightful place as its ruler. Instead, the kingdom was gone and Schulte had been forced to bring mankind back from the stone-age every *bloody* step of the way!

Where the hell was Dain?

Steady...

He topped off his glass before turning from the bar and tried to relax - settling deep into his favorite, leather-lined chair. Lownsbury's file still occupied a nearby living room table and he began to absent-mindedly leaf through it. He turned his reflection on the three rebels that had dealt him such a solid blow. Their propitious disaffection had proven to be unsettling - to say the least - and their timing could not be more inconvenient. Especially when success was so close.

So damn close, he could taste it!

He closed his eyes, pinching the bridge of his nose between his thumb and fingers as he did. Perhaps he had severely underestimated them.

Perhaps.

He had chosen them precisely because they were remarkable. Each possessing skills and a past that none of them fully understood. And so much the better that they were the absolute best in their individual fields. They had been exactly what he needed to achieve his goals.

Goals that he had been struggling to achieve for thousands of years.

Schulte sipped his drink, thinking of the three of them.

Captain Jack Sterling had proven to be an ongoing disappointment. Schulte had hoped - perhaps naively - for the Ranger's loyalty. It was always better to keep a dangerous man like Sterling in his own corner rather than running the risk of his disaffection. He had garnered his loyalty a number of times through the past, but Sterling's damaged mind had kept him unpredictable. Still, the Ranger seemed to be a timeless necessity. He would keep Sterling dangling until the time was right.

His prize star however was to be Professor Larimer Lownsbury!

Lownsbury's grasp on history and people of the past made him the one man on earth with the ability to track down the location of the one item he coveted the most: The long lost Alysian Artifact - *The Bracelet of Ra!*

With the power of the Artifact and his daughter at one side and Sterling on the other, he would be invincible to his brother. He could finally take his rightful place as emperor of the world.

He would again be a God!

Schulte sank his head back into the leather chair and sighed. How long had it been since he had last seen the Artifact?

It had to be close to four thousand years now!

Oh, but he could still remember the feel of it:

The ancient metal, hot in his hands as the tremendous power of the *Orb* became his to command. The intense sensation through his spine as it ignited the intensity of the Ichorous Elixir that flowed through him. The energy absorbing through his flesh - driving sizzling tentacles of electricity through every nerve ending of his body!

And - as the Elixir and *The Machine* connected - the infinity of the cosmos became revealed. *The Machine* opened the unending expanse of time and space, igniting the Bracelet and bringing it to life in his hands - granting him the power of a *god*!

The Ichorous Elixir alone, allowed travel through time with merely a visualization of where he wanted to be. Allowing time and space of distant realities to envelope him. Instantly conveying him to any location.

But the Artifact!

The Artifact enhanced everything magical within *The Machine*.

He inhaled deeply as he remembered. A small sip of his mellow nectar augmented his revelry and his thoughts again drifted to his daughter.

Samantha had been denied the joining of the Cratalis by Schulte's father as retribution for his mating with a *verboten*. As such, neither she nor her brother had the benefit of *The Ichorous Ceremony* and the infusion of the *Ichorous Elixir*. He was fully aware of his children's desire to find and possess that sacred *Cratalis*. Perhaps a passing fancy or necessary distraction, he really couldn't blame them - they were his children and just as covetous of the power it bestowed.

He closed his eyes, attempting to relax.

The Cratalis - Known through the ages by so many names: The Ichorous Elixir, The Chalice, The Holy Grail, *The Lapis Exillis,* its rumored survival had developed into tall tales of fiction. Presumed to be lost forever during the destruction of Alysia, Schulte had given up hope that the Cratalis would ever be found.

Relegated to mere legend, the Cratalis had eventually found its way into religious folklore and romantic fantasy, replete with fables of brave knights and secret sects. And this suited him just fine. He cared little about the Cratalis. Let it lay undiscovered. So much the better at controlling his daughter.

As was usual he questioned himself on this line of thinking.

Long ago, he had heard the stories that were passed among the Elders. Fables that had been bandied about that the sacred Cratalis had survived Alysia's destruction. It would be foolish not to stop and consider the potential for truth in the legend. Legends usually possessed elements of fact within their core and as such, he must assume there to be some veracity behind it.

This gave rise to another concern.

With Samantha bent on finding the Cratalis, would he be content with her possessing its awesome power? It would surely make them less vulnerable to problems such as they were dealing with now.

He dismissed this idea out of hand. It was far better to keep Samantha close to him and under his control. For someone as dangerous as Samantha, it would be absolute foolishness to ever let her join with the Cratalis. It was a circumstance he had to prevent at all costs, thus his need for Jack Sterling. Samantha could be unpredictable when her bloodlust took hold, but Jack could be controlled if you appealed to his sense of justice. But this meant he had to find the Cratalis first.

If it was out there.

If...

Schulte's impatience returned. Opening his eyes he stood - pacing, thinking.

What the hell was keeping Dain?

Schulte raised his glass to his lips, but he found the glass mysteriously empty. He poured another. He was becoming weary of these needless delays. He was eager to interrogate the professor - his need to find Samantha was becoming more agonizing with each tick of the clock. It was as if he could feel her calling to him from across time. He knew the consequences of their separation were growing dire by the minute. They had had the misfortune of separation once - long ago. It had nearly driven him insane and the devastation that had been wreaked upon his daughter was ungodly. Dain had been required to perform the *Rights of Restoration* on both of them. Not a pleasant undertaking.

The alcohol poured through his parted lips, portions of the brandy spilling down the front of his shirt. *"Damn it!"* He shouted into the empty room. He grabbed for a towel with his free hand, blotting at the rapidly drying alcohol.

'Where the hell was Dain?'

He struggled to regain his control.

Breathe.

A shimmer floated into the room and he felt his breath catch.

Dain had returned!

Schulte smiled smugly, he could almost taste the moment when the professor would realize what had happened. But when Dain materialized, he was empty handed.

Schulte blinked - unbelieving. His smile faded, "Where is the professor, Dain?"

Dain remained still and silent. No explanation could be garnered from his black, stoic face.

Schulte was at a loss. Dain had never been unable to complete an assignment before. This was so uncharacteristic of the giant man. Fury crept across the senator's face, but his voice remained hauntingly composed - a storm from the pits of hell began to brew beneath his calm facade.

"Where is the professor, Dain?"

The question was met with stony silence.

Schulte viciously flung Lownsbury's file from the table. Papers flew in every direction, snowing down into the living room. Dain shimmered in the afternoon light and the papers magically restored themselves onto the table.

"*Goddamnit!* I give you one job! One simple fucking job! And you come here empty handed?!" Schulte seethed, "Get the hell away from me, you monstrous son of a bitch!"

Dain vanished within a shimmering cloud, his head slightly bowed. Schulte dropped into his chair. He needed to think.

Think, damn it, think!

This was unlike him to be so emotional, but he urgently needed to find his daughter. With his fingers touching his forehead, he tried to focus. *How had Dain failed him?* It seemed impossible.

Schulte knew he must be losing his mind, for there was an answer. Only one reason why Dain would have been unsuccessful:

He had been intercepted by his brother; Ah-Vel. Ah-Vel had been there that night - they had seen each other. And Ah-Vel was the only one who could ever countermand a direct order given to Dain.

The meddling son of a bitch! He couldn't just tend to his own affairs.

Suddenly, a thought occurred to him.

This meant that Ah-Vel had an apparent renewed interest in the good doctor as well.

Now that was interesting.

Schulte straightened in his chair. This chain of logic soothed his emotions and calmer thoughts began to prevail. He needed to tread carefully with the professor now, lest he show his hand to his brother. He could not continue to suffer these setbacks.

Grabbing up Lownsbury's file, he began to sift through the assortment of paper that Dain had picked up from the floor for him. Calm returned and he reflected on what he had seen on the trip to Brooklyn with Dain to retrieve the professor. Lownsbury looked absolutely filthy as he staggered into that back alley. His clothes were torn. His jacket was tattered. His hair was overgrown and tangled and his beard was shaggy and unkempt. Schulte had never seen Lownsbury reduced to such a disheveled mess.

Indeed.

It was not in the man's character to have let himself go to that degree. Naturally, he would want to get cleaned up. Where would he go in order to do that? Where would any of us go to clean up and change into fresh clothing?

He would go home!

Leafing through the Lownsbury's file, Schulte found what he was looking for. His smile returned. "Of course," he said aloud - rising from his chair. It was an obvious destination.

Ah-Vel may have power over the Dark Man, but that was as far as it went. Ah-Vel or Hal, or whatever the unimaginative bastard called himself these days, would not encounter the same subservience with him as he had with Dain. Schulte would tend to this matter himself.

From the shadows of the living room, Dain watched as Schulte glimmered into nothingness - a long low groan escaping from deep within his enormous chest.

Twenty Two

Baghdad, Iraq; 2002

Doctor Jasmin Al-Bayati turned north on Omar Bin Yasir street and quickened her pace. She wasn't due back to work for two more days and she wanted to put as much distance between her and the hospital as quickly as she could. Her apartment was a brief two minute walk from the hospital and it was a walk she would have otherwise enjoyed. But the heavy military presence only served to unnerve her. She held her *Shayla* - a lightweight head scarf - across her face and kept her eyes down. Memories of her parent's death opened within her a fresh wound, and each uniform she saw was like a scathing dash of salt sprinkled in.

Turning down a small road that led to the front door of her apartment building, Jasmin breathed a little easier. The building was only a few brief steps away and inside she would find the peace and sanctuary she needed. Her breath caught though as a figure - dark and ghostly - seemed to materialize right next to her.

His arm wrapped around her and she felt the unmistakable jab of a gun into her ribcage. The man was tall and wet. He smelled of the river and days of unwashed filth. He spoke Arabic, but with a distinct accent. "Doctor," he said quietly. "I do not wish to harm you, but please do not force my hand."

Terror pounded through Jasmin as the memories flooded back - The Republican Guard, forcing their way into her family's home. Saddam's sadistic elder son - Uday Hussein and his friends entering on his heels.

The mysterious man that now held her seemed to feel the fear cascading through her and he tried to calm her as he led her into the apartment building. "I merely need your help Doctor," he whispered.

Jasmin was barely breathing as she opened the door to her apartment and her breathing ceased altogether when the stranger closed the door behind him. Turning her face to his, he said quietly - soothingly, "My name is Sterling, I am an American. I am not here to hurt you, but I need your help - *please.*"

The mystery of what Saddam's storm troopers had been looking for suddenly became clear as Jasmin saw her captor for the first time. Even unwashed and smelling of river water, the man was breathtaking. Tall and muscular, his dark, unkempt, soaking wet hair contrasted magnificently with the most amazing deep blue eyes Jasmin had ever seen. She instantly became lost in those eyes and it took her a moment to realize the stranger was in pain.

He nearly collapsed into her arms, but she steadied him and guided him to a back bedroom. He wore a lightweight tactical outfit that took some effort to remove.

As Jasmin helped the soldier undress, she couldn't help but notice his body. It was the form and shape of men that she had only seen and read about in magazines and she could not help but be moved as her fingertips touched his skin. She found herself sub-consciously outlining the contours of a body savaged with scars of battles long past as she helped him out of his clothing.

Sterling drifted in and out of consciousness as he tried to help Jasmin remove his clothing but eventually, even Jack Sterling yielded to the inevitable. His last vision before his mind checked out, was that of a beautiful, dark-haired woman jabbing a hypodermic needle deep into his flesh.

THE

MACHINE

Second Options

Part II

Twenty Three

"So this is how liberty dies; with thunderous applause."

-George Lucas

∞

Waset, Kemet - (Thebes, Egypt); c. 1550 BCE

Pen-Nekhbet was mind-numbed over the palace intrigue that was unfolding before him. His talk with Ka-Mose was unnerving yet - he had to admit - extremely captivating.

Ka-Mose resumed, "After Lord Tao's meeting with Apophi, I will travel north with a contingent of cavalry to secure my position as co-regent of Lower Egypt. We will then lead the Asiatic to their promised land. With the combined effort of both lands of Egypt, we will take control of the eastern edge of the Great Green Sea. There, the Asiatic will be seated strategically in the city of Sharuhen. Egypt will have its monuments and the delta returned to its people. And with the help of Apophi's people, we will stretch the hand of friendship across the sea towards Hattusa and beyond. We will expand Egypt's territory and be able to develop trade and protect Egypt at a price beneficial to everyone."

Pen-Nekhbet thought about this. It was a bold plan and one that seemed feasible, if not desirable. But he was still finding it difficult to believe that Lord Tao would have offered his consent, knowing the man's propensity for political indecisiveness.

"They won't all leave," Pen-Nekhbet stated boldly. No longer willing to accept timidity in his new position, he now took the attitude of advocating opposition to Ka-Mose. "The Asiatic, I mean. They won't all want to leave their homes to live in the Retjenu."

Ka-Mose smiled, "All their warriors will be gone. A second wave of our soldiers would be able to walk right into Avaris - unmolested. And from there we shall place a barricade from sea to sea. We shall blockade the road from Tjaru with checkpoints throughout the Wilderness of Sin. Never again for the Habiru to return. Any Asiatic left behind in Egypt has a choice to leave to Sharuhen, or be subject to levy."

"It will undoubtedly anger them." Pen-Nekhbet boldly demurred again, "Both the Kanan and the Asiatic will feel betrayed. We may not be able to maintain any of them as an ally."

Ka-Mose laughed loudly, "Our worst case is the retaking of our land with little fatality." - He shrugged with indifference - "Besides, Apophi will be unable to hold the Retjenu without our continued aid. And I have a secret weapon that Apophi desires. It will be his turn to acquiesce to Egypt."

Secret weapon? *What was Ka-Mose talking about?* But Pen-Nekhbet's questions were to remain unasked.

Ka-Mose suddenly sat upright in his chair and leaned in close. Pen-Nekhbet could smell the alcohol on his breath. It was only serving to accentuate his own queasiness.

"You are now given an incredible opportunity Pen-Nekhbet," Ka-Mose breathed wickedly. "You can bring around powerful reform that will sanctify both our peoples. Your name will be forever remembered as the bearer of justice. Not only for your brethren here in Egypt, but for all of mankind. You shall be a champion of justice for everyone; your name will come to be the very definition of the word."

"*Justice.*"

The word echoed in the silence that now hung between them.

Baghdad, Iraq. Many centuries later.

Doctor Jasmin Al-Bayati looked down on the man with concern. He was bathed in sweat and writhing in the throes of fever - and nightmare. She checked his pulse. It was bounding; strong and fast. And given the circumstances, extremely disconcerting. She wrung a fresh towel of excess water before wiping the sweat from his naked body.

Jasmin was surprised the man had survived his injuries this long. He could damned near be classified as a medical oddity. The gunshot wounds he had sustained were healing incredibly fast. Faster than she had ever seen in all of her years as a medical doctor. She had had her doubts that he would survive with the damage he had received. But his rate of healing was unprecedented. Far beyond remarkable.

He was however, still maintaining a dangerously high fever that was showing no immediate signs of weakening and regardless of the speed of his wound recovery, the fever still held him dangerously close to meeting Allah.

Springing from the shadows the previous evening and holding her at gunpoint, he had begged for medical help and sanctuary. He said that he was an American soldier that had tangled with the palace. She didn't know what trouble the man had caused, but he had been shot numerous times before he had escaped. The Republican Guard had obviously failed to find his body and was now on a serious manhunt. Many of Saddam's storm troopers had accosted a good number of her colleagues in the hospital - threatening each with death if they were caught harboring the fugitive.

Jasmin had sealed her own fate by allowing the stranger sanctuary in her small apartment. If he was found by the Republican Guard, they would both be executed. But what else could she have done? He had been badly injured. Jasmin knew that the man had massive internal injuries, but the type of surgical procedure he needed was impossible to undertake outside of a well equipped hospital. And even then, his chances of survival would have been slim at best.

At that point it was merely a waiting game. Waiting for him to finally succumb to his injuries; leaving her with a body she would need to deal with. Not the first in her lifetime and likely not the last.

But every minute that ticked by, the man seemed to be recovering on his own and at a fantastic pace.

Unbelievably fast.

If it wasn't for his damned fever.

Jasmin wrung out another water soaked cloth. Rubbing his fevered body and forehead, she did her best to quiet the fevered man as he thrashed. His cries increasing in volume. If her neighbors heard him, they would certainly alert the authorities and then there would be no further recovery.

For either of them.

He cried out again.

Jasmin rinsed the towel and placed its cool surface across the stranger's forehead, hoping to break the fever.

"Please be quiet," she whispered in English. Hoping some conscious thought might remain that he could hear her pleading.

But the man continued to thrash about, his body pouring sweat. While in his sleep, his fevered mind replayed visions and memories. A single word echoing from his cracked, dry lips:

"*Justice...*"

Twenty Four

Mansfield, Connecticut; Modern Day

The water - hot and ferocious - pounded onto Lownsbury's bare back. The scorching, liquid fingers, seared through his flesh - teasing its way slowly into his every aching muscle. Its welcoming touch lulled him ever deeper into its dreamy, euphoric embrace.

He was home. He could breathe. He was finally at peace.

Peace.

He had so longed for peace.

Peace from the terror of Samantha. Peace from the horrors he had witnessed in seventeenth century Salem Village and then again - only moments ago - on the unforgiving streets of Brooklyn.

Peace even, from the debilitating effects of his travels through time.

Peace.

How magnificent to simply let the blistering water of tranquility - hot and refreshing - wash the cold stink of perdition from his tortured body. To simply drift into the inner depth of his own mind.

Yes - to drift into that inky, alluring abyss where time and conscious desire abandoned him. Leaving in its wake a pathway for the sweet, intoxicating embrace of serenity.

Of sanity.

The heat of the water enveloped him further in its rejuvenating mist as he drifted into his own inner sanctum. A construct of his own creation. A retreat within his own mind he had developed as a child soon after his mother had died. A safe harbor from the horrors of life. And of death. A place where only he could dwell and where he could bar the gates to the demons that plagued the real world.

Peace.

There - within that safe haven - he could find the balance between the light and dark. Between good and evil. Between terror and tranquility. He breathed deep. Inhaling the steam and basking in its rejuvenating shroud.

Suddenly, a welcoming fragrance - as of perfumed ambrosia - captivated him; delighting his senses. Sending him further into his dreamy void. A void where nothing mattered. Nothing could harm him. Nothing could destroy the ecstatic exhilaration that bound him.

Into a sweet, dreamy confusion Lownsbury drifted. Drifting until the peace that enveloped him was all consuming - swallowing him in its euphoric embrace. Swaddling him with the feeling of delirious warmth and elation. His senses overflowed with that delicious fragrance and he prayed it would never end.

So deep into his sub consciousness Lownsbury had drifted, that he had not yet realized that the shower was no longer running. His weary mind did not immediately grasp the significance - the implication that he was no longer alone.

Lownsbury's mind continued to float in and out of conscious thought - allowing fate to intervene unmolested as his world floated into surrealism. A happy wonderful, ambrosia filled dream.

Peace.

But was he dreaming? Was the sweet, ambrosial aroma so intoxicating to his senses that he was unable to awake?

He determined that he must be dreaming, for he had lost any will to fight against the feeling of sleep - against the irresistible allure of warmth and peace.

Peace.

Yes - dreaming, and perfectly so. Dreaming that two sets of arms gently lifted him from the bottom of the shower. His euphoria held fast and he remained unalarmed at the presence. As if it was all just meant to be. As if it were his fate to be beguiled to another's desire, so long as his peace was to remain.

He managed to open one very tired eye and through the narrow, hazy eyelid, he envisioned two exquisite young women, gently bringing him to his feet within the shower. Their bodies visible; barely concealed beneath the sheer clothing they were draped in. A decorated thin rope, classily tied about their waist was their only adornment. Their thin veils - sensuously draped across the tip of their noses - highlighted elegant blue eyes. Eyes that radiated the naked tenderness of servant girls. Perfect in their simplicity and purpose.

Together, they began to tenderly towel him dry. Beginning with his freshly deloused head and moving down his arms. His body. Their hands reaching between his legs, touching him soothingly.

Intimately.

Their bodies bathed in that wonderful, sedating perfume of the gods.

His body reacted to the two young women and within his dream filled state he was neither embarrassed nor ashamed of his reaction. It too seemed as natural as their very existence. As natural and welcome as the warmth that continued to envelope him. Lownsbury's clouded mind simply allowed the two of them to continue their task as he basked in their exquisite touch.

Their task finally finished, the two young women wrapped a fresh towel around his waist and cinched it tight. With a gentle nudge, they steered him from the bath and into his bedroom. Tantalizing him with delicate, feathery movements and an enchanting elocution.

Once in the bedroom, the two of them expertly caused his knees to bend and - with very little effort - softly lowered him to the floor, pushing his head low. The movements seemed such a natural thing and he was as putty to their desires; allowing them to manipulate him as they saw fit.

He could feel a gentle breeze blow across his naked flesh, kissing his body with its silky touch. That sweet, intoxicating ambrosial fragrance wafted through the room again, further clouding his already clouded mind.

With great effort, Lownsbury raised his head.

Standing in front of him was the most beautiful woman he had ever seen. Like the servant girls that remained genuflected to either side of him, the lower half of her face was draped with a gentle sheer covering. Her eyes captivated him with an indescribable exquisiteness that glowed with a combination of sensuality and refinement.

And of wisdom.

Her piercing emerald green eyes reminded him of Samantha, but her aura was filled with a grace and perception that reached far beyond that of Samantha. He instinctively knew that Samantha was as a child compared to this woman. Lownsbury was enchanted, for surely an angel stood before him

An angel from God.

She must be.

The woman radiated such love that Lownsbury believed her to be an angel. He was so captivated by this woman that he came to the realization that he *was* in love. For the first time in his life, he felt genuine love and he delighted in it because of her. He rejoiced in the love of being in her presence.

Peace

She was modestly adorned, a colorful, lightweight blouse draped elegantly across her form. The fabric was sheer and offered scant adequacy in concealing her breasts; perfect in their composition and form. And though she radiated such distinct sensuality, it was underscored by an undeniable class and nobility. She portrayed neither shame nor embarrassment at her exposure but rather, seemed perfectly natural in her element.

Tinsel of gold and silver was laced elegantly throughout her long blonde hair. Romanesque braiding allowed gentle wisps of hair to escape along the side of her head, draping sensually down either side of her face, further accentuating her beauty. Lownsbury could see a genuine smile that reached deep into her viridian eyes. The love she radiated filled him with an easy calm, cascading him deeper into his own dreamy state.

Peace

The two young women to either side of him, gently lifted him to his feet as the angel reached out her hand.

When she spoke, it sounded like English - but it was of such a distinct dialect that he could not immediately understand her. It was lilting, musical. And her voice further convinced him he must be dreaming. Once again Lownsbury was reminded of Samantha, but this woman's accent was far more defined. Every syllable was a symphonic delight.

"*I am queen Evalana of Alysia, Larimer,*" she sang.

Alysia? Where or what was Alysia? Lownsbury thought briefly.

But in the end, it mattered not. For it was simple joy just to hear this angel speak his name.

"*Take my hand, Larimer.*"

Lownsbury was captivated. He could not resist. He did not want to resist. Her will was his command and there was nothing he would deny her. He knew that.

As he touched Evalana's hand, the two young servant girls surrounded her as well. Each reaching to touch her. Servant girls who appeared just as elated at being in her presence as he was and he understood their feelings perfectly. He joyfully let her arms envelope him.

Lownsbury suddenly noticed a small pinpoint of light - intense and bright - focused on a small corner of the bedroom wall. *How odd*, he thought. What was that? Where had it come from?

The light occupied his thoughts, focusing them. He blinked against the intensity.

Suddenly, the light grew larger. Rapidly growing and engulfing the wall, moving around them as if it were eating the room where they stood. Swallowing the floor, the walls. As though a superficial reality were vanishing to reveal a new one that lay beneath.

The effect was startling and it took his breath away. The speed with which the room was eaten away was overwhelming. A disturbing feeling of vertigo washed through him as an entire new surrounding suddenly enveloped them.

The room in which they now stood was like crystal. It was stark. Not really white, but more as glass. It was austere; only a small, padded, table top bench occupied the room. It was a thin table that reminded him of an operating room. Light emanated from all around them - from the ceiling and walls - with no real defined fixture.

Several men and women, all of them extraordinarily tall were there as well. Each wore tight fitting clothing, deep blue. As with Evalana and the servant girls, sheer fabric draped their faces - hiding all but their eyes.

As a group, they bowed as one. Deeply, and with unmistakable respect and reverence at the sudden appearance of their queen.

Queen Evalana spoke. Her voice - soft and musical - sang to them, *"Please resume."*

Everyone in the room just as purposefully righted themselves.

Ambrosia wafted through Lownsbury's senses again as the two servant girls guided him to the table, directing him to lay back upon it. Anything they wished was his command as his head swam through the delightful fragrance.

The two servant girls disappeared from his view as the attendees of the room immediately took their place on either side of him.

Evalana was suddenly next to him, too.

"Where am I? Why am I here?" He managed to ask.

"Please relax Larimer," she sang to him. "We cannot have you wandering throughout time like this. You would prove a hazard to all of mankind."

Lownsbury - content in his fragrance filled euphoria - believed that there was nothing Evalana would not receive if she asked him. Even now - believing that he was facing his own death - his life was hers for the taking. And he gladly accepted that fate now, just as she wished.

An angel from God.

Peace.

Suddenly she was gone.

Lownsbury could see the masked faces of those that remained. He could feel needles going into his arms and legs. He could feel the catheters in both his front and back. Small tubes were forced down his throat. But all of it done so gently, that Lownsbury barely noticed.

It all felt so natural.

Before the remains of his conscious mind vanished, he thought he could hear Evalana's voice. Musical and enchanting. As if she were right next to him.

"Goodbye, my child. Until our fates again entwine. May wisdom guide you."

Larimer Lownsbury closed his eyes and drifted dreamily - warm and content - into that deep, black, ambrosia filled abyss.

Twenty Five

Baghdad, Iraq; 2002

The sun was high in the sky when Jack Sterling finally awoke. He didn't know where he was. His body was clean and naked. A large bandage was wrapped tightly around his abdomen. His head ached. He needed water badly.

On the nightstand sat a tall glass of water and Sterling grabbed it up - sniffing it before gulping down the contents.

He made a quick search and found his weapon in the nightstand drawer.

The magazine was gone, the chamber - empty.

Struggling to his feet - his head swimmy - Sterling staggered to the bedroom door. He was alone in a small apartment. A large plate glass window in the small living room looked out on a city that Sterling recognized immediately as Baghdad. Memories played across his consciousness, but they were vague and disjointed.

Sterling made a cursory check of the apartment and the view from each window. There did not seem to be any activity in the street. It seemed that he was relatively safe. He also noted that there was no other escape from the apartment than the front door. He tried to find some clothes to put on, but all he found were women's clothing and nearly all of it was several sizes too small. The owner was undoubtedly petite. A vague memory of a beautiful woman standing over him surfaced, but faded quickly into the fog.

A familiar warming sensation ignited above his heart sparking other memories. Indistinct pictures from an unclear past. He closed his eyes trying to remember when a noise outside the door drew his attention. He slithered as quietly as he could behind the door just as keys clattered in and around the lock and the door opened.

A woman wearing a long, colorfully patterned dress, with a matching, bright blue, lightweight *Shayla,* draped across her head entered. She had a sack in her arms. As she was closing the door behind her, she noticed Sterling standing there. His berretta in his hand aimed straight at her head.

Sterling tried to speak, but his mind was still foggy and he was having difficulty in forming words. His mouth was dry and his lips smacked as he tried to open his mouth.

The woman barely appeared startled and turned her back on him as she walked into the kitchen. Sterling followed her, staggering, confused, his gun still trained at the back of her head.

As she pulled items from the bag she had carried in, she said in near perfect English, "I see no reason for you to continue to wave that gun around at me. We both know that there are no bullets."

Sterling lowered his arm almost thankfully. He was still dazed and it had taken all of his energy to keep his arm out. "Where am I?" He managed.

Her tone was matter of fact - almost cold, "My name is Doctor Jasmin Al-Bayati. You are in my apartment inside of inner Karada in downtown Baghdad. You took me hostage three days ago suffering from multiple gunshot wounds. You are on a large amount of painkillers and antibiotics and you are severely dehydrated."

She was suddenly in front of him with a large glass of water. "Drink this," she said. "Slowly."

Sterling took the offered water thankfully and - ignoring her advice - nearly downed it in one gulp.

Reaching into the bag again, she pulled out a simple pair of lightweight male pants and a shirt. She brought these over to Sterling, "Let me help you with your clothes."

Sterling realized he was still naked and shook his head, trying to relieve some of the grogginess. He noticed he was still holding the gun and laid it carefully down on an end table, making a mental note of where he had laid it. Leaning against Jasmin, he lifted each leg in turn as she helped him into the pants. And then, into the shirt.

Jasmin said, "I have to go into work. You are safe here, but do not leave. The Republican Guard is still searching for you. These clothes belonged to a cadaver that had been brought in last night. If you do not shave, you will blend in well."

"Thank you," Sterling said meekly - trying to remember why the Republican Guard would be looking for him. He was suddenly exhausted and needed to sit down.

Jasmin helped him back into bed, "You need more rest, Mr. Sterling. When you awaken, we will talk. You are safe here."

Jack Sterling was asleep before his head hit the pillow.

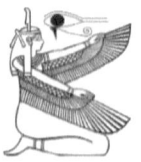

Twenty Six

Waset, Kemet - (Thebes, Egypt); c. 1550 BCE

Imhotep's coalition** would never allow for the leading of an army into Avaris without provocation," Pen-Nekhbet said. "Your plan will be met with stiff dissention from within the palace."

Ka-Mose merely smiled in response.

Pen-Nekhbet was finding it difficult to think clearly through the foggy effects of the hangover that plagued him, but he knew he had been handed a baited hook. "What do you want from me?" he asked guardedly.

Ka-Mose sat back, exhaling heavily. He snapped his fingers and a servant boy again magically appeared to refill his mug.

Pen-Nekhbet planned on declining with a shake of his head and a hand over his cup. He was still unable to stomach the sweet after-taste of over-indulgence that haunted his palate. But Ka-Mose took the carafe - refilled his own mug - and sat the decanter on the table between them. With a wave of his hand, he sent the boy on his way.

"Your first assignment as the new Herald will be the overseeing of supplies and personnel for Lord Tao's travel down river to Avaris. You shall confirm that everyone is where they are supposed to be and see to provisions and ports of call."

Pen-Nekhbet was well aware of his duties, but he did not interrupt.

"I shall require passage of my courier. Place him on one of the provision barges, out of your way."

Pen-Nekhbet noticed that his statement was not a request. "And just who is this passenger that will be accompanying us?"

Ka-Mose set his mug on the table, "In the city of Gebtu, a temple official named Teti awaits. As you dock for supplies, allow him to board. He will accompany you as far as the city of Iunu - to the Temple of Ra - where he will disembark. No questions asked, no lies told."

Pen-Nekhbet frowned as he tried to grasp the significance of the request.

The Temple of Ra was one of the oldest temples in Egypt, residing deep within Lower Egypt's boundaries and Asiatic territory. Situated within the city of Iunu, the Temple of Ra was the greatest archive of knowledge known to the world, and was aggressively protected by nine very powerful priests. Rumored to be immortal - as most of the high priests were - they were rarely seen, and never meddled with - not even by the Asiatic.

What might Ka-Mose need from the Temple of Ra that he thought this person - *Teti* - could achieve? Pen-Nekhbet wondered.

No questions asked, no lies told.

Ka-Mose continued, "Also, when you finally reach the port at Avaris, wait at the dock your first night for the second bell. A Kanan named Joshua will approach you to give you information to bring back to me."

"I am to be a spy's courier?" Pen-Nekhbet asked incredulously. "I will not perform in secrecy of his majesty."

"I assure you there is nothing clandestine, Pen-Nekhbet. Joshua has important information from Apophi concerning troop placement and numbers that are vital if our plan is to succeed. Tao is aware, but he must remain in position of plausible deniability."

Ulterior motive.

Ka-Mose sipped his wine in thoughtful silence for a moment, "Once he has given you his information, I want you to give Joshua this correspondence," he said - pulling a small jar from the folds of his linen. The container bore the personal seal of Ka-Mose. He handed it to Pen-Nekhbet.

Pen-Nekhbet turned the jar through his hands, studying the detailed glyph of the seal. Curious as to what the message inside contained - he asked, "What does it say?"

Ka-Mose tilted his head between sips, "That's a rather bold question, wouldn't you say?"

"You have asked a lot from me, my lord. Conscription into a potentially seditious line of action - based solely on your word - may not be beneficial to my well being. I mean no offense, but if candor is what you encourage from me, this moment seems an appropriate one to insist upon reciprocation. Insisting to know the details of your arrangement with a Kanan spy seems altogether deserved."

Ka-Mose nodded in thought, "Very well. I am instructing Joshua's team to scout the Wilderness of Sin and the tribes of the Retjenu for their weaknesses to ensure success of our plan."

Pen-Nekhbet paused long moment before asking, "Is that what my entire role in this shall be?"

A heavy, wine laced breath escaped Ka-Mose. He cocked his head in that familiar way, and smiled, "Well there is one more thing that I ask. It is simple. I wish for the princess - Sitkamose Ah-Mun - to accompany you. She has never seen our monuments in the north; this would be a unique opportunity for her."

Princess Sitkamose Ah-Mun - of the family of Ah-Mose - was Lord Ka-Mose's only daughter. Pen-Nekhbet had heard the stories. Rumors really. But he had never met the princess. Her name brought with it curiosity and intrigue among most of the people. Fear even from those who had claimed to have met her. Rumors had it that she was extraordinarily attractive, with eyes that could penetrate a man's soul. Possessing a seductive charm that none could resist, she could enslave even the strongest to her darkest desires. It was told that she was as deadly as she was enchanting. A witch that delighted in the sexual perversions of the damned.

Pen-Nekhbet knew that these were just rumors and he knew how rumors could grow with each passing telling. But a shiver of delightful anticipation ran through his spine nonetheless. He would finally have the opportunity to meet the enigmatic princess and discover for himself the truth of her sorcery.

Pen-Nekhbet swallowed, "I am neither a child's guardian nor tour guide. I cannot guarantee her safety on a diplomatic mission."

Ka-Mose laughed into his near empty wine mug, "I appreciate your attempt at chivalry, Pen-Nekhbet. But *your* ability to protect my daughter is the furthest of my concerns."

Twenty Seven

Mansfield, Connecticut; Present Day

Lownsbury snapped awake. Hours had ticked by and the sun was high in the sky. He looked at the bedroom clock; it was nearly two thirty in the afternoon.

These last few days had been an emotional roller coaster. His body and mind ultimately had had enough and after his shower, he had collapsed - naked and wet - into his bed. Exhaustion finally taking its toll. The need for a shower and a decent night sleep had been long in the making and his soul finally felt as refreshed as his body.

The shower.

A recollection sparked in his mind, but only faintly. Perhaps more a feeling, triggered by a heavenly aroma that seemed to linger delicately on the outer reaches of his senses. The name Evalana touched his memory and he struggled for a moment to maintain a grasp on a beautiful dream, but it faded to nothing.

Making his way to the kitchen, he made himself a very large breakfast consisting of everything he could find in the fridge. He was starved of nutrition and everything his eyes fell upon quickly became devoured. He left nothing behind.

Lownsbury dressed with new clothes and a fresh sports jacket. He pulled the door open on a small safe he had stowed in the back of his bedroom closet and retrieved a small bundle of cash from inside. Ten thousand - modest but adequate.

He also pulled a small .38 special revolver from inside the safe - along with spare ammunition. Hopefully he wouldn't need the gun, but underestimating Schulte was not a mistake he ever cared to make again - he would rather be safe than sorry.

It was nearly five o'clock before he finally sat down at the kitchen table and began to work on his time phone. It had been completely disassembled by the town clergy of Salem Village when he and Samantha had been taken prisoner - and consisted of the intermingled parts of two disassembled phones. It was barely held together with the fabric of his jacket lining he had cannibalized while imprisoned there. It was beyond serendipitous that the phone had still been able to transport him as much as it had.

It had also been extraordinary luck that Lownsbury had been able to find all of the pieces - reassemble the phone - and flash out of his prison cell without Samantha. She was extremely resourceful and absolutely deadly and it had taken all of Lownsbury's cunning to free himself from her long enough to flash into time.

He considered Samantha and all that had transpired with their stay in Salem Village. For as diabolical and murderous as Samantha was, Lownsbury had been willing to gamble his life to save her from existence in that hellacious prison. In fact, he had fought his better judgment in that contemplation. It was as if she had held a spell over him - her sexuality so honed as to be irresistible.

He suddenly remembered that Captain Sterling had been alone with Samantha at the compound during her interrogation. Sterling had admitted to being amorous with the beautiful assassin prior and this suddenly called into question the captain's motivations. Could Jack Sterling be fully trusted knowing the power Samantha seemed to have over men? He himself had barely managed to break free from Samantha's spell. Could Captain Sterling be as strong?

It was an interesting thought that he needed to consider.

With slightly shaky hands, Lownsbury turned his attention back to his time phone in a careful attempt to unwrap the bundle. He desperately needed this phone so he could flash to another time and place. Somewhere that Schulte could not find him - to give himself time to consider his next move. With all that had transpired - and now with the deep suspicion regarding Captain Sterling's state of mind - fading into anonymity was no longer an option. He had research to do on Schulte if they were to be successful. There was more to the senator than any of them knew. And if his hunches were correct, Schulte and his daughter were far more powerful than any of them had realized.

As a history professor, the past held a singular fascination for him. But his time spent in Salem Village with Samantha had taught him that no matter his destination - or his reasons for going - even the most seemingly benign of places was not without its dangers.

He needed to think and the time to do it.

The phone was still fragile - the pieces held together only by that strip of worn and grimy cloth. Lownsbury found a stash of screws in a baby food jar in his utility closet. Rummaging through the collection, he found a couple of small screws that weren't quite the right size - but he thought would likely work in keeping the phone together.

He steered his mind to the events of the previous night and the escapade at the café. His mourning for his mother had subsided, but it had left questions in its place. He remembered Hal from his childhood. A kind man that had taken him in for a short while until Lownsbury could be properly placed into a foster home. He couldn't remember exactly how long he had stayed with Hal, but he remembered the time had been brief. After his placement, he never saw the big man again - until just last night.

And he looked exactly the same as Lownsbury remembered.

The biggest question from the previous evening's events had to be Hal's ability to know Larimer as his adult self and the lack of surprise that Hal had shown in seeing him. He seemed to know that Lownsbury was in danger or had potentially compromised the mission. He also was fully aware that Lownsbury was not in his own time period. That necessarily meant that Hal was conscious of his time travel movements and his mission.

But how could he possibly know that?

Hal was definitely mixed up in all this and Lownsbury decided that his first task would be to find out what he could about his childhood savior. His mind was clearing - he was revitalized. He had a purpose. His optimism was on the rise once again. Perhaps he would see what he could find out about the man whom Lownsbury knew only as Hal.

A familiar, delicate odor delighted his senses. An intense wave of déjà vu suddenly cascaded through Lownsbury. His head became swimmy with the power and force of the sensation and he stumbled slightly. Confusion clouded his judgment as he struggled with the feeling.

The phone case pulled apart - just as he was removing the soiled cloth away from the body of the phone - and the jumble of mess inside spilled out onto the dining room table. He made a grab at keeping all the parts of the phone confined to the table but in his confused state, he swatted one of the pieces off of the table and it clattered to the floor with a sickening crack.

"Bloody hell!" Lownsbury exclaimed aloud.

As quickly as it came, the feeling of déjà vu passed. Lownsbury breathed deep as his countenance steadied.

Ensuring that all the remaining pieces were stationary on the table, he scrambled to his knees in search of the runaway piece. His worst fears were realized when he found the remains of a fractured display screen. The glass was ruined - a large crack ran the full length of the screen. Green striations crazed away from the crack and a random piece of plastic fell away as he picked the remains from the floor.

Lownsbury was drained. His emotions had peaked and he could only stare helplessly at the damaged jumble of parts. His plans of conducting research - much less starting a new life somewhere innocuous - had suddenly vanished. He had not been a big fan of the time travel experience to begin with but now that the option was gone, he suddenly felt confined. Closed in. And once again, hopelessly alone.

"How can this get any fucking worse?" he said aloud in exasperation.

Turning around at that moment, his question was answered.

Twenty Eight

Baghdad, Iraq; 2002

S terling was standing at the window, sipping hot tea from a cup as he stared out at the city street that ran in front of Doctor Jasmin Al-Bayati's small apartment. He had removed his shirt. The large bandage wrapped around his waist was warm in the stifling little apartment and the shirt made him uncomfortable. It had been just over a week since he had been shot breaking out of the Republican Palace. He had made remarkable improvement and although his ribs and stomach were still very sore, his mind was focused and clear as he planned his escape from the city and his return to the United States.

The front door opened and Jasmin entered, returning from her shift at the hospital. Sterling was not surprised, he had seen her walking up to the building. But he still had his Berretta at the ready.

His mind had cleared from the painkillers, but his memory was still largely incomplete. Jasmin had returned what was left of the ammunition. It was only two rounds and Sterling desperately hoped he would not have to use them. If the need arose for their use, they would undoubtedly not be enough.

He still had his tactical knife - a twelve inch blade he called '*Beast*' - and this he kept strapped to his calf.

"You should not stand so close to the window. You may be seen," Jasmin said softly - admiring Sterling's physique. Her eyes traveled the length of his body until their eyes met, causing her to modestly divert her gaze.

Sterling smiled and took another sip of his tea. His eyes searched the street once more before letting the curtain fall back into place. He followed Jasmin into the kitchenette. His attention was drawn to something that he hadn't seen before - a small plaque that displayed a grouping of Egyptian hieroglyphs. Sterling looked at the ancient symbols for a long moment until Jasmin noticed.

"I bought it at a bazaar in Cairo last summer. It's supposed to bring luck," she explained. "I find it mesmerizing. I wish I knew what it actually said."

Sterling blinked and sighed, "It is a partial royal titulary of a pharaoh from long ago. It says he was the possessor of the power of Ra, granting him everlasting life."

Jasmin raised her eyebrows, impressed, "You are very surprising, Mr. Sterling. You can read Egyptian hieroglyphs. Not very many people in the world have such knowledge."

Sterling blinked and looked at the floor - confused. "I don't know how I know that. I guess I must have read it somewhere."

Jasmin pulled her *Shayla* scarf from her head and let her hair fall around her shoulders. Her eyes were alive and she smiled warmly at Sterling, "I see you are feeling better, Mr. Sterling. It is good you are up and thinking clear - yes?" Truth be told, Jasmin was absolutely amazed at Sterling's recuperative ability. He was healing at an incredible rate. Faster than she had ever seen before.

"Yes, thank you Jasmin," Sterling said - truly grateful. "Please call me, Jack."

The woman had taken care of him, putting herself at great risk by doing so. A fact not lost on Jack Sterling. Jasmin was a beautiful woman, inside and out. She was in an uncharacteristically jovial mood and Sterling wondered why.

"I have something for you," she smiled - her eyes dancing.

Reaching into her bag, she removed an identification card. The picture was that of a man, close to Sterling's age. Although his height and weight were less than Sterling's, the face was similar enough that he could pass. The writing was in Arabic.

"Your new name is, Ali Abdul Al-Nassir," Jasmin said gleefully.

Sterling took the card. He shook his head, "I can't tell you what this means to me. You have been very kind, Jasmin. How can I ever repay you?" He could almost guess the answer to his question and somewhere inside of him he felt a tinge of regret in asking. "How did you get this?"

Jasmin turned away from Sterling, her eyes had suddenly turned sad. Taking a seat at the small kitchen table, she drew in a slow, deep breath before releasing it into a heavy sigh. Slowly - as she searched for the right words, she began a confession:

"I remember when Saddam went to Kuwait. I was just a little girl, but I remember how terrible he was. He had already killed so many that had opposed him that most of the country were gripped in fear. He had always been a sadistic beast. But after the Americans beat him in Kuwait, he became worse.

"There were stories that were whispered back then that if Saddam were to go to Kuwait, the Americans would put an end to him and his tyranny. We were all so excited that the Americans would come. Even though we couldn't say it, the people in my village wanted Saddam dead. We were praying that Americans would finally kill him and free us so that we could live without fear.

"We cheered in our village when Saddam announced he was to go to Kuwait. We were not cheering for him though, we were cheering that we would soon be free of the monster and his evil sons. That the Americans would save us. It was a long wait - it seemed like an eternity. But finally, we heard that the Americans would be coming."

She turned her eyes to Sterling, "We could see the smoke from the battle as they drew close. We were waiting, ready to welcome them. Some of us were crying tears of joy and I remember thinking *'we are saved.'*

"But, the Americans never came. They gave up. Even though Saddam was defeated, they gave up. But then the radio said that if *we* stood up against Saddam ourselves, they would come back and help us. But it was a lie. Many of us stood up against Saddam, but he had become more evil. He and his sons killed so many of the people. He killed them horribly with his poisonous gases. But the Americans never helped. They turned around and went home."

Sterling vaguely remembered the *'Road of Death'*. He recalled how it had become a political football and how the decision had been made to quit before reaching Bagdad. They had routed Saddam from Kuwait and that was all that had mattered to some of the politicians. Sterling shook his head. As a soldier - trained to kill - it was hard to understand the thinking of politicians sometimes. Their *'Cover Your Ass'* strategies usually killed more people than they ever saved.

119

Jasmin continued, "One day - when I was still a very young girl - several Republican Guards came to our house. Saddam's son – Uday - was with them. We had thought we were to be liberated and because of this, my father had voiced displeasure against Saddam. They forced him to watch as all of them used my mother - and then me. Uday then slit my parent's throats in front of me and just left me to watch them die."

She sniffled - breathing deep before continuing, "A neighbor called my father's brother and he found me there and took me away to England. I have family there that had escaped Iraq and had taken professorships at Oxford. I worked very hard and studied to become a doctor. I thought I could come back here to help my people." - She shook her head in dejection - "But life is wretched. They do not approve of educated women here and every day it gets worse." She brushed away some imaginary crumbs from the table, "Now that the Americans have been attacked, I know that they will come here again. They will destroy things and promise life will get better. But then they will elect a new president and he will have a different idea about what should be done. We cannot trust them. They will leave us again and then Saddam and his sons will become worse. Their egos bruised, they will become intolerable. Eventually they will forbid me to be a doctor and I will be killed for my western education."

Silence settled between them. After a long pause, Jasmin finally drew a deep breath, "A man came into the hospital last night, he had been in an accident. He spat in my face as I tried to treat him. He told me I was a worthless, pig-loving whore. It is something that happens often." She looked up at Sterling - her eyes seeking redemption. "I went back to his room later and injected him with drugs and took his identification card." A tear ran down her cheek, her emotions on overload. She looked down at her hands. "I do not feel bad about killing him. He was a despicable man. I am just sad that Iraq is no longer home to me." A long pause – then, "If we can get to Kuwait city, my uncle will get us aboard a freighter to America."

Sterling sighed and put his hands on Jasmin's shoulders. She put her cheek against his fingers. He could feel her tears and couldn't help but be moved. The moment sparked a vague recollection of another woman. It was a distant vision he couldn't quite remember, but one that seemed important.

Suddenly hundreds of distant thoughts clouded his mind at once: The Republican Palace; the slaughter of his team; a corrupt United States senator; a sudden ability to read the Egyptian symbols on Jasmin's kitchen wall; a bloody princess in a battle to the death; the Black River; Cithimay; Ipu; *The Cratalis*.

"We belong together."

The memories played and replayed, rolling together into confusion. Their meanings vital, but so unclear as to be meaningless.

The Cratalis!

"We belong together."

Then - just as quickly as they had came - it were as if a switch was flipped and the memories evaporated, leaving Sterling dazed and confused. He closed his eyes and breathed deep. His anxiety dwindled.

Finally - he kissed the top of Jasmin's head. A sweet fragrance of lilacs played across his senses clearing his mind and bringing focus. "It will be extraordinarily dangerous just to get to Kuwait," he said softly.

"When they find out what I did, I will be butchered in the street. I do not ask for anything more than an opportunity."

Sterling nodded. He had asked her to risk her life by saving his and she had sacrificed it entirely. There was no way that he could not now save hers.

Twenty Nine

Waset, Kemet - (Thebes, Egypt); c. 1550 BCE

Pen-Nekhbet stood behind a small table on the dock directing the loading of supplies and personnel to the three large barges docked a short distance offshore. Egypt had recently purchased four of these barges from their *Fenkhu* brothers in *Kubna*; a large city specializing in ship building along the shores of the *Great Green Sea*. Mostly used to transport supplies to cities up and down the Black River, the barges could also navigate the choppy waters of the Great Green and could also be modified for dignitary travel as need be. Each had a rower's hold beneath the top deck in which VIP's could travel in the privacy of a small berth, protected from the brutal Egyptian sun.

Four reed transport boats were busy running crew and provisions from the dock to the royal barge - *Wild Bull*, and the cargo barge - *Northern*. The flotilla throughout the duration would be under the direct command of Admiral Apy and his second in command, General Khafra. The transport boats would remain with the barges during the voyage for ship to ship communication, deliveries and docking at ports of call. The loading of provisions had been proceeding at a steady clip. Lord Tao was scheduled to arrive at any time and thus far, they were on schedule. Ka-Mose's daughter – Sitkamose - also had yet to arrive.

Glancing out across the river, Pen-Nekhbet could see a large amount of activity on the *Wild Bull* as the crew readied the ship for the arrival of his majesty. The morning sun was already intense, causing the river to sparkle under its brilliance. Pen-Nekhbet shielded his eyes from the glare. He suddenly noticed a large contingent of *Medjay* approaching; Nubian mercenaries hired by the palace as royal bodyguards. They were widely known for their intimidating size and menacing demeanor. There were at least a dozen soldiers clustered tightly together in formation - walking across the scorching plaza towards the dock. Their armament dazzled just as brightly as the river under the searing sunlight. As they drew near, Pen-Nekhbet could see they were surrounding a person wearing a full length cloak with a hood pulled deep over the head. He could not see the persons face, but he easily recognized the cloak the person wore:

It was the same mysterious person he had seen several nights previous at the Heb Sed festival!

His breath caught in his throat.

The Medjay split into smaller numbers, some following the cloaked figure and a young, dark-haired, royal service maiden as they boarded a docked transport boat. They quickly made their way to the deck house of the boat and away from the intense rays of the sun. Only a couple of the Medjay followed the pair onto the boat to guide them safely to their barge. The rest took positions on the dock, turning away any further supplies or personnel attempting to board.

Pen-Nekhbet stared after the mysterious figure that had haunted him during the festivities a few nights previous. The figure was obviously the princess, *who else could it be?*

Even unseen, her aura was captivating. He helplessly wondered what she looked like and hoped he would have a chance to find out. So enamored Pen-Nekhbet had become with the mysterious figure, that he didn't hear the Medjay captain's words as he approached table.

"I'm sorry, please say that again," Pen-Nekhbet stumbled - clearing his head.

"I present the princess, Sitkamose - of the royal family of Ah-Mose."

Pen-Nekhbet blinked, "Yes, of course. Uh, she will bunk aboard the *Wild Bull*."

The head Medjay nodded his acceptance and a runner set off to deliver the instructions to the boat captain.

Pen-Nekhbet was left to wonder about the veracity of the rumors he had heard. He watched in silence as the boat quickly left the dock to deliver its enigmatic cargo to the royal barge floating offshore.

The voyage north had been as clockwork.

Lord Tao had punctually arrived amidst a flurry of pageantry; wrapped in a platoon of bodyguards, color guard and even a few palace trumpeter's. Tao - with his palace steward – Imhotep - following dutifully behind - finally managed to board several transport boats. The entire entourage set out towards the *Wild Bull, en-masse.*

The dock had finally been cleared of supplies, courtiers and other personnel awaiting passage to the royal barges parked offshore. Pen-Nekhbet - the last to board - was finally able to make his way to the main barge, *Wild Bull*. Finding his cramped quarters, he sat down heavily in the rope hammock that would serve as his bunk.

He breathed a heavy sigh and rubbed his tired eyes.

Coordination of the launching of the royal flotilla had been tedious. The sun was already a couple of hours old, but the schedule had been managed well. He felt some gratification that the beginning of his first assignment had gone so well, but a feeling of apprehension still plagued his mind.

What was Ka-Mose's plan?

Ulterior motive.

He closed his eyes for a short cat nap, enjoying the alluring caress of the ship as it drifted into the flow of the river for its journey north - down the Black River to Lower Egypt.

As Ka-Mose had promised, a short man calling himself Teti, had been waiting for their arrival as they pulled into the dock at *Gebtu* for more supplies. He carried with him a medium sized package - wrapped in white linen - which he hugged tightly to his body. Across his chest, he wore the traditional sash of a Lector Priest.

It was well known that Lector Priest's would make themselves available to any person or event that required their services; performing rituals and prayer for funerals and ceremonies. They were said to be keepers of secret wisdom and magic spells, often said to be stored in the pages of their *Book of Spells*; such as what Pen-Nekhbet assumed Teti was carrying - grasped to his chest.

However, he had never seen such restlessness from a Lector before; Teti was making furtive glances all around the dock and it was clear that he was anxious to get to his ship. He was a spectacle of nervous twitchiness; clenching and unclenching his fists around his bundle as his eyes moved ceaselessly and constantly asking when they would be underway…

"As soon as provisions are replenished and all passengers and crew have made their way back to the ships," Pen-Nekhbet answered curtly with a disdainful glare.

Pen-Nekhbet was still uncertain about this entire affair and was a bit aggravated that such a tedious bore was now in his care. Even if he was a Lector Priest. He put him on one of the smaller cargo ships - as Ka-Mose instructed: *"Out of the way."*

The blessings of *Ah-Mun* were kind and Pen-Nekhbet did not see Teti again until they had neared the port of Iunu. Yet - neither did he see the princess, Sitkamose. He had purposely stationed himself aboard the *Wild Bull* hoping to meet the rumored enchantress, but Sitkamose stayed to her quarters.

Pen-Nekhbet's thoughts now shifted briefly to the pretty young palace nurse - *Ipu* - whom he had met a few nights earlier on the opening night of the *Heb Sed*. He and Ipu had become quite close since that evening, spending as much time together as possible over the last couple of days. Pen-Nekhbet knew their connection was strong, perhaps even strong enough to consider making a family.

But what was it about the cloaked princess - a person he still had yet to lay eyes upon - that was so alluring?

Pen-Nekhbet watched the water of the Black River slip by the prow of the barge. A distant, uneasy feeling remained. A creeping awareness, begging the question, *"Was he doing the right thing?"*

Thirty

Mansfield, Connecticut; Present Day

The front door to Lownsbury's apartment was open and his nosy neighbor, Mrs. Brown was standing on the landing. Her mouth was agape with a pronounced look of surprise. In her hand she held a jumble of freshly delivered mail. Her astonishment balanced slightly with recognition. "Professor Lownsbury," she managed. "I wasn't expecting to see you."

Lownsbury closed his eyes. He had forgotten he had asked Mrs. Brown to collect his mail while he was away on his lecture tour. Any ounce of optimism he had left suddenly dropped through the floor. His worst fear had been realized - he had been seen. If she told anyone of this meeting - *anyone* - it could compromise everything. There was no way of knowing if Schulte would discover this chance meeting in the timeline. If he did, it could be disastrous. He hoped he could return from this mistake but without the time phone, he saw no hope in correcting this blunder.

He needed to be casual now; conversational; not arouse her suspicions. Lownsbury knew that he undoubtedly appeared different. His already thin body had been emaciated even further from his prison stay in Salem Village. Not to mention his newly shaved head. She had seen him only recently and would unquestionably reason something was amiss.

"Mrs. Brown," Lownsbury said with as much warmth as he could muster.

He could see the surprised look on her face and remembered his midnight barbering. He thought quickly - running his hand across the top of his head, "I was in Bridgeport and had an unfortunate accident with a piece of gum. I thought I could sneak back up here quickly and get back to the tour with none the wiser. My apologies for surprising you."

The explanation might be adequate for his new shaved look, but did nothing to hide the marks still left from the beating he had endured at the hands of Samantha.

He decided not to offer one.

Mrs. Brown beamed and blinking, shook off her shock. "That's quite all right, Professor. I didn't mean to surprise you either."

She handed the stack of envelopes and flyers over to the gaunt man, her warmth returning. "Here is your mail."

Lownsbury took the stack from his neighbor after quickly scooping the remains of his time phone into his jacket pocket. He absent mindedly leafed through the correspondence, hoping that Mrs. Brown would excuse herself. But she remained firmly planted.

"So, how is Mr. Brown, then?" He finally asked with barely veiled annoyance.

The neighbor took no notice of Lownsbury's irritation; the need to gossip more pressing. She took the nicety as an invitation to settle into a living room chair. "Henry has been very busy," she smiled. Finally - somebody to talk to - a captive audience.

"Hmm," Lownsbury muttered - now on the search for an opening to get the woman out of his home as nonchalantly as he could. He continued leafing through the envelopes, trying not to be openly rude.

"Henry is being called to the Historic New England Museum in Boston." She smiled sideways, "You know, to try to settle the big controversy."

"Hmm," Lownsbury repeated. A water bill, an electric bill, junk mail. Lownsbury reminded himself that he really didn't need to go through the bills here anymore, but he couldn't think of an alternative. His time phone - the lifeline to *The Machine* - was damaged. It was all he could think about at the moment. Besides, leafing through mail was more interesting than listening to Mrs. Brown drone on about the life and times of her and her insurance adjuster husband.

"Anyways," Mrs. Brown continued - undeterred. "That Paris box has raised a lot of eyebrows and now Henry is staying in Boston until he can either figure out how the hoax was done, or pay the client his insurance money."

"Hmm," Lownsbury said again. Another grocery store circular, a magazine invoice, junk, junk and more junk.

"Paris box?" he asked unthinkingly. The words had escaped him before he realized he was prolonging her stay.

Damn! He sat down on the sofa and began to put on a pair of shoes he had taken from his closet. Perhaps the act would encourage her to cut her visit short.

He needed to leave.

"That's right. Oh surely you've heard about it on the news," Mrs. Brown continued cheerfully. "It's been all over the television."

She looked at Lownsbury for affirmation. But he was still at a loss, concentrating solely on a problem that had suddenly arisen with his shoe horn. He needed to get this woman out of here.

Finally - she broke the silence, "You know? The reverend in the Salem Witch Trials? I know how keen on history you are."

Mrs. Brown suddenly had Lownsbury's full and undivided attention. "*Parris's Box?* Are you referring to the *Reverend Samuel Parris*?" Lownsbury sat forward - his left shoe undone - the shoe horn all but forgotten at his heel. "I'm afraid I have not kept up with the local newscasts lately, please indulge me Mrs. Brown - What of this box?"

Mrs. Brown was suddenly alive. Her story aching to be told. Her hands moving as fast as her tongue. There were moments in his neighbors narrative in which he forced her to slow down - but the more she spoke, the more Lownsbury realized an ever increasing tale of tragedy was in the making.

Thirty One

The Black River Delta, Lower Egypt; c. 1550 BCE

The voyage of the royal flotilla of King Seqenenre Tao of Upper Egypt had been going well. They had nearly reached their destination port of Iunu - near the eastern mouth of the tributaries of the great, Black River delta. But the sun had set and the winds had shifted, hampering progress. At this time of year, it would have been dangerous for the large ships to enter the channels of the delta in the dark so they had battened down for the rest of the evening. There to await first light in order to launch transports to guide the larger ships through the narrowing channels downstream, towards the port of Iunu. The respite would also give Apophi's information couriers time to announce Tao's imminent arrival to the palace, further downstream at Avaris.

The hot weather of the day was rapidly yielding to the cooler temperatures of the encroaching night. A cool river breeze was now a welcome relief to the still sweltering temperatures from below deck and Pen-Nekhbet took a few moments to enjoy an evening stroll topside. Staring out across the dark river, he could see the torchlight of sentry positions at the port of Mennefer - a short distance to the west from where they were anchored. The torches that outlined the two supply barges floating nearby were diffused by the dark water below.

A noise shook him from his ruminating and it took a few moments for his eyes to adjust. Turning in the direction of the noise, one of the transport boats could be seen - the oars quietly dipping into the water. The small papyrus boat was slicing rapidly through the river, silently making its way toward the port of Mennefer. In the dimness, Pen-Nekhbet could make out the silhouette of someone sitting aft - clutching a white linen bundle.

It was Teti - Ka-Mose's courier. Setting out on his own. His mission held tight to his chest. He was obviously not waiting till light - choosing instead to steal away in the night.

What was in that package to risk so much by navigating the river in the middle of the night? What was in Teti's lector book that he would guard it so vigorously? Was it even a lector book? Pen-Nekhbet had to admit he had not even seen what was beneath the linen wrapping.

And what was worth the risk of drawing the attention of the Asiatic sentries at both Iunu and Mennefer? Sentries that were undoubtedly keeping close watch on Tao's flotilla for any inappropriate behavior.

Pen-Nekhbet remained silent. Watching in resignation as the transport boat vanished silently into the night.

Thirty Two

Mansfield, Connecticut; Present Day

Mrs. Brown sat with Lownsbury in his living room telling him the story of a Wayland, Massachusetts man named Robert "Bobby" Hatfield that had come across a large antique box in an old dilapidated barn that he was razing on his property. The box was more than three hundred and twenty years old with a date imprinted on the exterior of 1690. It was covered in leather, adorned with leafy decorations that had been stamped across its exterior and a faded coat of arms emblazoned across the front. It had been discovered locked with an ancient padlock that had not been opened in nearly three hundred years. The lock frozen closed.

The description of the box gave Lownsbury a chill. He remembered going through that very box in Parris's parlor room the night he absconded with the parts to make a phone. He and Samantha had arrived in Salem Village with two phones. Both had eventually been disassembled by Parris. Lownsbury had had to take enough parts from the two phones to make one complete phone.

The very parts that were now in shambles inside his coat pocket!

He remembered the ornate box that held those parts. He could remember the coat of arms vividly:

The knight's helmet adorned with crown and plume, the shield that boasted the busts of three unicorns and the sprouting of the French fleur in the background. An eerie feeling ran through him.

Mrs. Brown told Lownsbury that the Wayland, Massachusetts man had taken the box to the local historical society to determine its value. The historical society established that the coat of arms was that of the Parris family and - due to its age and the location near Reverend Parris's last known residence - the box had likely once belonged to the Reverend of Salem Village; Samuel Parris.

Lownsbury recalled that it had been Reverend Parris and his family that had been at the center of the entire Salem Witch affair in 1692. It had been his preaching on witchcraft that spawned the hysterics - fueled by others in political power - in an attempt to control land and to do away with those that stood in their way. Lownsbury and Samantha's unearthly arrival had unintentionally set in motion the entire witch trial incident.

The historical society had brought in experts from several museums to authenticate the box. Each had offered their opinions creating a consensus that the box was genuine. They had confirmed that the lock was contemporary with the box and it appeared to have been unopened in all of that time. The contents would certainly be an intriguing and historical find and could shed ongoing light on the dramatic events that had unfolded in that little town during that fateful year. Mr. Hatfield decided to cash in on his new find and demanded a million dollars for the purchase of the relic. The New England Historical Museum in Boston had been prepared with a large money donor at the ready. Everyone had been overjoyed and equally excited by the exquisite find. With the ancient box in hand, the New England museum put the box through a series of dating tests and X-rays.

That was when the controversy began.

As the X-ray pictures began to detail the unopened contents of the box, an impossibility seemed to be contained within. Wrapped within the folds of an ancient textile - perhaps a handkerchief - was the indistinct outline of a modern day item. It was an impossibility and the pictures were quickly explained away as ghost images; traces of an antique with similar characteristics.

It was determined that the lock must be cut and the box opened to retrieve the contents. Once the lock was cut away from the hasp, it was sent to a lab for dating analysis to determine how recent the lock had been used and just how old it was. The box was opened amidst much pomp and ceremony - with the press pushing their cameras to be the first to see what treasures this historic find held. What was discovered inside became the center of a raging argument.

Among the delicate folds of an ancient tapestry, were the aged pieces of an obvious modern day pistol combined with a jumble of other modern junk. The museum was at a loss, unable to explain how a firearm from the modern era could be found in a confirmed closed box from the seventeenth century. It was concluded that a mistake must have been made somewhere.

An expert in firearms was called in from Kansas to determine what kind of pistol it was. The answer only served to spread gasoline over the firestorm that had been brewing. The expert had determined that the disassembled gun was a modern day Glock 19, 9mm pistol.

Another expert from the Glock factory was flown in from Austria only to confirm that it indeed was a Glock 19. The age could not be readily determined so it was sent to a lab in New Jersey for further testing. Thermo-luminescence dating was inconclusive, but preliminary findings indicated that the gun was more than three hundred years old - give or take twenty years. It was promptly returned to the museum.

The museum donor who had purchased the box for the museum cried foul and demanded his money be returned. Mr. Hatfield refused and - with his lawyer in tow - had made a statement pronouncing that testing was confirmed concerning the legitimacy of the box and the fact that it had never been opened. Therefore, the contents of the box were immaterial in relation to the authenticity of the box itself. Due diligence was the burden of the buyer and it had been performed to the buyers satisfaction - prior to purchase. Any issues arising thereafter fell within the scope of *caveat emptor*; (buyer beware.)

An intense legal storm was taking place; the litigation cloud was forming. The issue was garnering national attention and Henry had been sent to Boston as the adjuster to determine what role - if any - that the insurance company would take.

With the national attention mounting, it was guaranteed that Schulte would hear of the issue. It would take very little for him to put two and two together and determine that one of his time travelers had gone to Salem Village. It would not be a great effort to see if Samantha was still there.

This was beyond tragic as far as Lownsbury was concerned. He no longer had an option; his plans of researching Hal would have to wait. It was a certainty that Schulte would now be able to locate his daughter once he heard this news.

Which he was certain to do.

Lownsbury's pragmatic mind took hold and he reasoned that if Mrs. Brown was able to tell the tale of this enigmatic pistol and that it was now being held in the Boston museum, meant that Schulte had not yet found the Parris box in the past. Of course that would presuppose that Schulte would even care about it after retrieving his daughter.

Time was of the essence. It was a foregone conclusion that Schulte would travel to Boston to look at the gun to see if it was Samantha's. Lownsbury needed to get there first.

But what would he do if he did determine it was her gun? How would he be able to let his team know? He no longer had a time phone. He guessed he could get to Colorado or send them a message somehow. But that would take time.

He had to act fast and sitting here visiting with his nosy neighbor was a waste of time he didn't have. He pulled the shoe horn from his shoe, quickly tied the laces and stood up. His tone surprisingly forceful and demanding, "I have to borrow your car and your cell phone, Mrs. Brown... *Now!*"

Thirty Three

Shuwaikh Port, Kuwait City; 2002

Sterling and Jasmin could see the shimmering blue water of Kuwait Bay in the horizon - soon after crossing the border checkpoint in Um Qasr. With each step of the way, the fear of discovery diminished. The pilfered ID worked well through each checkpoint and Sterling and Jasmin breathed a collective sigh of relief when they finally saw the lights of Shuwaikh Port across the bay.

They had decided to declare marriage early on to prevent unwanted scrutiny. Something they had discussed prior to stepping aboard the bus to Um Qasr. Muslim law would still be heavily enforced - even in American friendly territory and they saw no sense in pressing their luck.

Jack Sterling could describe the trip south in one word; Beige. He had grown so tired of the bland tan of the desert that he longed for just a little dab of color. Even the small homes and tiny towns were the same color as the desert.

The sun remained high in the sky during their trek south to Kuwait. It was oppressively hot. But once they arrived at the docks in Kuwait City, they could feel a gentle, cooling breeze drifting in over the ocean. Even the smallest movement of cooler air was a wonderful respite from the brutal, desert heat.

Jasmin quickly found her uncle's moderately sized cargo freighter. As they made their way towards the vessel, a tall, thin, dark-skinned man approached them. His overly large eyes searched them, head to toe and back again - quizzical. Far from handsome, the man's rugged features spoke of a harsh life at sea, yet his smile suddenly became warm and kind as Jasmin pulled open her *Shayla* - briefly showing her face. He recognized his niece immediately.

"Jasmin," he said with fondness - but without embrace. His Arabic was quick and clipped, but Sterling was able to follow along with most of their conversation. "It is so good to see you."

"Thank you for your help uncle. This is Ali Abdul," she said - introducing Sterling. Although Jasmin used the alias she had given him, Sterling knew from the look in her uncle's eyes that the old sea captain wasn't fooled in the least. What the sailor lacked in beauty, he obviously made up for in wisdom. "This is my uncle, Captain Fasir," she finished.

The two men shook hands. Sterling noticed that Fasir's hands were like steel. His grip; a vice.

"You are welcome aboard my ship," he said. "But, I ask that you stay below decks in your rooms. My crew would not understand our arrangements. My steward will deliver food to the both of you." - A pause - "And Jasmin…" - he focused a stern look on his niece - "…You must be discreet." His words were laced with a mixture of worry and warning.

"Yes, uncle," she acquiesced.

Sterling discovered in the short time he had known Jasmin, what her uncle had likely known for years; having lived and been educated in the western world, Jasmin had a mind of her own and this did not mesh well within strict Muslim culture.

Their visit was brief. Captain Fasir summoned his steward - a young teenage boy of perhaps fourteen years - who led them from the docks, up and onto the ship. The boy never spoke a word as he brought them quickly below deck to a long hallway with cabin doors to either side. He showed them to two rooms midway down the hall, the doors directly opposing each other.

After opening the doors, he left them to their own. Although they had separate rooms, they chose to huddle together inside one of the cabins as they waited in eager anticipation for the ship to finally take to sea. The rooms were small and cramped. But it did nothing to stifle their brimming elation. Jasmin was overjoyed and Sterling was happy to see her smile. He believed it had probably been years since she had ever smiled and he thought that the look suited her very well.

They bided their time talking and telling stories of each other's lives. Things one could only tell a stranger or a very close friend. From

Jasmin's family anecdotes, to workplace shenanigans - as well as loves, won and lost.

Jasmin asked Sterling about his past, but his thoughts were still hazy. All he could remember was that he was a soldier. Always had been. And he had absolutely no recollection of childhood.

As night fell over the shimmering desert port of Kuwait, Sterling saw how stunning the setting sun could be when reflected in a lonely, beautiful, Iraqi girl's eyes.

It was several hours later when they finally felt the throbbing pulse of the massive engines as they came to life, deep within the bowels of the vessel. The low vibration only seemed to heighten the growing need that pulled at them. It released an overwhelming emotional sense of relief that manifested into a mutual aching desire.

As the ship left the Gulf of Oman and headed into the Arabian Sea, they could feel the weight of all they had been through evaporate. That first night - in a state of near euphoria - they found themselves in each other's arms. Releasing weeks, months and even years of oppressive tension and pressure that had been growing. Jasmin lived her first night of freedom with uninhibited delight.

Thirty Four

Mansfield Connecticut; Present Day

Boston was less than two hours away but to Lownsbury, the trek up I-90 was maddeningly slow and he again lamented the disabled condition of his time phone. He knew Schulte would be seeing the national news broadcasts and realizing what had occurred. More than likely he would head to Boston as well to confirm the story.

Lownsbury didn't know if travelling to Boston was the right move or not, but he had to see for himself. A sinking feeling was telling him the obvious answer and he was positive that the gun in question was the one that Samantha had brought to 17th century Salem when Lownsbury had transported them. He had not had the opportunity to retrieve all the evidence before escaping. Now that error was coming back to haunt him. He also knew he had to get word to Jack and William, but how could he do it fast enough? Getting that gun out of the museum needed to be his first hurtle. Without a time phone, it was all he could think of doing.

Lownsbury taxed Mrs. Brown's car, pushing it as fast as he could.

Mrs. Brown wiped her hands on the dish towel as she scurried to her front door. Visitors were a welcome break in her monotonous and never-ending housekeeping chores. Opening the door she was greeted by the warm and charming smile of a well-dressed, upper class, middle-aged man. Mrs. Brown was immediately smitten.

"Good afternoon," the gentleman caller said. "I am sorry to disturb you Mrs. Brown, but I was looking for Professor Larimer Lownsbury. Would you happen to know where I can find him?"

Mrs. Brown was captivated. The fact that the gentlemen knew her name without them ever having met, escaped her. "Oh, you just missed him. He left here only a few minutes ago."

"Oh, how unfortunate," the man said with obvious disappointment. A hopeful look returned, "My name is Senator Ted Schulte. Would you happen to know to where he took off? I wouldn't normally ask such a personal question, but it is imperative that I find him."

"Oh, my," Mrs. Brown blushed. "I thought you looked familiar." - She pulled the door wider - "Please come in Senator, I can certainly tell you where he dashed off to."

"*Excellent.*" The tall, impeccably dressed man's charming smile widened as he stepped through Mrs. Brown's doorway, "*Excellent.*"

Thirty Five

The Black River, Lower Egypt; c. 1550 BCE

The return trip home was about to be underway and once again, Pen-Nekhbet was the last to board.

The voyage thus far had been eventful and quite busy. So busy in fact, that he had put the image of Teti - stealing his way to shore in the dead of night towards Mennefer - into the back of his mind. And only briefly had he wondered if princess Sitkamose had made it off the ship. If visiting ancestral monuments had been her goal, Mennefer would have been the port to disembark. Pen-Nekhbet had not seen her - ensconced in her cloak or otherwise - emerge from her quarters during the voyage. The palace handmaiden that had accompanied her had been seen often however - delivering food and beer to their quarters. He decided that he would determine the princess's status once he made it back to the *Wild Bull.*

In fact, there had been so much going on in attending to Tao's meeting with Apophi, that Pen-Nekhbet hadn't had the time to attend to much with flotilla affairs either. Instead, he had placed Admiral Apy in charge of supply inventory for the preparation of their return trip.

Attending the negotiations with Apophi and Tao had been educational in many ways. Ka-Mose had been correct; Tao and Imhotep were in attendance with their emotions. The wearing of the *Sekhemty* and the fawning delivery of worthless gifts conveyed a hollow impression. Optics that were blatantly designed to create a narrative that the look of disdain on Apophi's face indicated he did not share.

Pen-Nekhbet was gratified to see however, that the lengthy scroll of advanced mathematics he had transcribed several seasons earlier, was part of the offering. Lord Tao had ordered him to sign his name to the scroll in honor of King Apophi just several weeks earlier. He remembered that it had been a lot of work transcribing the papyrus from the older work. The original was said to have been created by the god *Ta-Huti*, himself.

What surprised Pen-Nekhbet more than anything else though, was that Prince Apophi did not seem to share the same Kanan look that the rest of the Asiatic possessed. Instead, Apophi held a strong resemblance to the crown prince - Ka-Mose.

Very odd.

In fact, it was downright eerie.

Pen-Nekhbet also noticed how Apophi seemed to regard both Tao and Imhotep as fools; offering sarcastic remarks about Tao's crown; his ridiculous attempts at symbolism over substance, and even delivering a backhanded remark about Tao's beloved hippopotamus pool back in *Waset*. Little was spared Apophi's derision but the remarks were so subtly veiled - and Tao and Imhotep were so self absorbed - that the comments remained wholly unheard. Pen-Nekhbet was finding it difficult to stomach much more of Imhotep's pomposity, Tao's ignorance and - even less - Apophi's sarcasm.

The meeting concluded that first evening in the gardens where refreshments were served. The dignitaries were invited to quarter in the palace with the remaining crewmembers bunking aboard the ships. Pen-Nekhbet excused himself from his majesty to attend to affairs aboard ship and promised a swift return to the palace once admiral Apy and his crew of the flotilla were attended to. He had quickly made his way back to the docks; his unspoken motivation to remove himself from the political theatrics and await the foretold arrival of Ka-Mose's spy - Joshua. He hastened his pace to get back to the dock before the ringing of the second bell.

The ringing of the bell was a system of security checks used by the Asiatic sentry regiments. Established to denote segments of the night, each sentry would contact distant ports and other sentry units throughout the town and river bases - letting each know that all was well with a single chime of the bell. The first bell had ringed earlier, marking the setting of the sun. The second bell was due to be rung very soon.

Pen-Nekhbet made it back to the dock just as the second bell sounded its single strike. Replies could be heard all along the river bank and throughout the city proper. He did not have to wait long before a stocky man was seen walking up to the dock area. Stout, but short. He was a head and a half shorter than Pen-Nekhbet with the typical dark hair and features that were undoubtedly Kanan.

Pen-Nekhbet stood as the man approached. "Joshua?" He said - (pronouncing his name, *Yawshway*)

The man nodded and immediately began to talk. His accent was thick and Pen-Nekhbet had to listen closely to what he was saying, "Long live lord *Ka-Mude*," he said quietly - using the Kanan pronunciation of Ka-Mose.

Pen-Nekhbet eyed him suspiciously, "What say you?"

Looking around - displaying the same twitchiness as that of the lector priest - Teti - he said, "A large contingent of chariot archers left yesterday on the march to the city of *Tjaru*. Apophi has kept to his word with troop training focused for our planned campaign into the *Djahy*."

Pen-Nekhbet remained quiet, listening.

Joshua took another long look around the dock to make sure they were alone before continuing - but what he said was a bit of an unexpected shock, "Please assure prince Ka-Mude that the great pyramid of the ancients is being stocked with the jars as he instructed."

Pen-Nekhbet lifted his eyes. Had he heard that right? With a tilt of his head - he asked, "Jars?"

Joshua looked at Pen-Nekhbet for a second and shook his head. He was apparently just as mystified. "Honestly, I do not know," he said - shrugging his shoulders. "I was hoping you could tell me. The pyramid chamber is now packed with many of these very large jars," he said - miming the size of the jars with his hands at about waist high. "We cannot fit another. The jars are filled with wine - certainly turned - and affixed with a stopper that holds a combination of metals. They are all connected together with metal ribbon, attached to two large bars that extend into the ceiling of the ante chamber. I do not understand the arrangement myself, but if I were to guess, it appears that the wine may be an offering to *Ra*?"

Pen-Nekhbet had no idea what the jars of wine and its odd tethering were about, but expressing his own ignorance would not serve a position of strength his office supposedly purported. Joshua's question was met with stony silence. Reaching into his carry bag, he pulled out Ka-Mose's small, sealed jar. "Here are your orders from the prince - I shall deliver your report."

Joshua observed that Ka-Mose's seal on the jar was intact then nodded once and disappeared into the night, leaving Pen-Nekhbet to ponder what he had learned.

Jars of wine stored in the great Pyramid of Ra?

Tethered together with metal ribbon?

What could possibly be the significance?

Ka-Mose did not seem like the sort that would occupy a lot of time in sacrificing to the gods, so what was his purpose?

What did it all mean?

Pen-Nekhbet thought of Tao's meeting with Apophi again; it was difficult to believe that Tao still thought that Apophi would simply subordinate his own crown to him. The two men appeared to be playing entirely different games and Pen-Nekhbet was becoming more concerned that Tao was not in full knowledge of Ka-Mose and Apophi's arrangement. The meeting between Tao and Apophi held no indication that a joint military effort into Kanan was in play.

This meant that in order for Ka-Mose to move Egyptian troops towards Avaris for the purpose of joining forces with Apophi, some other motivating factor would need to be put into play. There was something going on, but Pen-Nekhbet could not begin to fathom what it could be.

But he was determined to find out.

Thirty Six

Boston, Massachusetts; Modern Day

Professor Lownsbury!" the curator to the New England Historical Museum gushed as he crossed the foyer of the Otis mansion, his hand outstretched. "I got here as fast as I could, Professor. You understand we closed almost two hours ago."

The Otis mansion sat at the foot of Beacon Hill - adjacent to the Old West Church - and was a testament to the craftsmanship and design of the architect - Charles Bulfinch. Built in 1767 for Harrison Gray Otis and his wife Sally, the Otis family name became synonymous with early Boston political influence and social affluence. The Otis family home now housed the local Museum of American History.

Lownsbury turned his attention from the ornate woodwork adorning the room he was admiring to return the handshake, "Thank you, Stephen. I wouldn't have requested your audience if it wasn't an emergency."

As a history professor at the University of Connecticut, Lownsbury had the pleasure of visiting nearly every museum of natural history in the United States. And most of the east coast museums had become acquainted with the eccentricities of Larimer Lownsbury. His controversial views and historical perspectives flew in the face of what many considered the political propagandists that posed as historians. And his name preceded him in most of the institutions of critical thought. He had made very few friends in his passionate elucidation of historical fact. Stephen Andrews was one of those few.

"No trouble at all," Andrews answered cheerfully - looking at his watch, "As it turns out, I have another appointment within the hour here. How can I be of service?"

Lownsbury frowned, "Pardon me Stephen as I dispense with decorum and arrive to the point. I understand you have a relic that has created quite a spectacle?"

Andrews nodded, "You mean the pistol found in the Parris box. Indeed it has, Professor - indeed it has."

Lownsbury cleared his throat, "My neighbor is Mr. Henry Brown of the Atlantic Insurance Group - insuring the purchase - and he thought I might be of value in helping clear up the matter."

Andrews was taken aback, "With all due respect Professor, this hardly constitutes an emergency. Your visit could surely have waited till morning."

"I do apologize but I assure you, time is of paramount importance in this matter," Lownsbury retorted - ignoring his own pun. "May I see this item?"

"Even if I wanted to show you the gun, it is impossible - The FBI confiscated the weapon. I was informed that the item may have been used in the commission of a crime and they are currently performing forensic analysis to determine this."

"So, the gun was operational?" Lownsbury asked - surprised that warrants had been issued for confiscation of defunct property without cause.

"Oh, good heavens no," Andrews laughed. "It is obviously far too old for that. The only surviving portion of the gun was the polymer stock. But you know as well as I that constitutional considerations have all but vanished here. The government can do as it wishes with no reason or mandate. Now tell me professor, what are you really doing here?"

Lownsbury sighed, his entire demeanor projecting his dejection. "Perhaps it was a pipe dream. When I had heard that the Parris Box had been discovered, I thought..." - his voice trailed.

Stephen Andrews consoled, "It seems that this meant a lot to you." - A pause as he considered his next few words - "I will tell you what I can do. Let me show you the box. There were other things inside that box far more interesting than a Glock 19."

Thirty Seven

The Black River, Lower Egypt; c. 1550 BCE

After a lot of deliberation - and with the consideration of the politics that seemed to be in play - Pen-Nekhbet made up his mind that he needed to reveal Ka-Mose's plans to his majesty - Seqenenre Tao. It was his duty to do so and it was Lord Tao's right to know.

However, Tao had been drinking far too much during his stay in Avaris and his indulgence had taken its toll. Tao was now sleeping it off below decks. It would be hours before he was able to converse. Pen-Nekhbet would just have to wait.

In the meantime, Admiral Apy had asked Pen-Nekhbet to join him aboard the supply ship, *Northern* to inventory supplies for the purpose of plotting a route back to *Waset*. It was discovered that the beer supply had dwindled faster than anticipated and they would need to dock sooner for replenishment than originally expected. With Tao otherwise inaccessible, Pen-Nekhbet decided to meet with Apy.

They had originally wished to get clear of Asiatic territory - to prevent paying tariffs - but it was evident that it was not going to be a possibility. They decided they would need to dock at the port of Mennefer to replenish.

However, they had left the city of Avaris late so by the time they entered the river proper, the sun had long set. The air had turned chill and a thick fog had rolled across the river - severely limiting their vision.

The port of Mennefer was still a good distance away and with their vision so hampered, they decided to batten down and wait until morning light.

Suddenly a frantic shout arose from the lookout of the *Northern*. Arriving on deck, Pen-Nekhbet found Admiral Apy and the lookout directing a small contingent of row masters that were attempting to capture a derelict transport boat that had been found drifting. Darkness - combined with the soupy mist that floated above the river - hampered the salvage operation. It became further complicated when it was discovered that the *Wild Bull* was also adrift. Its path set floating back down river.

Pen-Nekhbet and Apy shared a concerned look.

What had become of General Khafra and the guards of the royal barge?

Admiral Apy and Pen-Nekhbet suddenly had a dire urgency to discover the disposition of the king and his royal entourage. They immediately commandeered the salvaged transport boat and a small contingent of four guards. They gave orders to the captain of the guards that another contingent was to follow. Pen-Nekhbet and Apy began hastily making their way through the murky haze to the *Wild Bull*.

Climbing aboard the royal barge, Pen-Nekhbet slipped on something slick and nearly fell. In the torch light, a massive pool of dark red became visible. Each of them shared questioning looks as to what the deck could be covered in. Disbelief in what they were seeing was finally followed by a realization.

Blood!

It was everywhere - seeping into the cracks and soaking its way across the planks. Their sandals slurped with each step in the gruesome fluid. The stink that wafted from the ship was like a slaughter house, causing Pen-Nekhbet's breath to catch.

"General Khafra!" Admiral Apy shouted. But only silence answered him. The ship was like a tomb.

Pen-Nekhbet put a hand on Apy's arm, indicating that he should refrain from shouting and that they should instead, proceed with stealth.

Admiral Apy nodded.

Suddenly, a muffled scream was heard from below deck!

The guards immediately launched into action - hunkered low, their bows chambered and drawn. Their khopesh sickle swords were sheathed but were within easy reach as they swarmed to the stairs that led to the lower levels. They were followed closely by Apy and then Pen-Nekhbet.

Arriving below deck they really didn't know what they were seeing. Like an overflowing, morbid honeycomb, gore dripped from everywhere. In the amber glow of the torchlight, they could see that the walls were painted in that unmistakable red. As it was above deck, the lower deck was also covered in entrails and bodily fluids - the mutilated bodies of men and women were scattered everywhere. Pen-Nekhbet barely recognized Sitkamose's palace maiden, lying in a bloody, misshapen heap in the far corner.

They were startled even further when they realized that a figure was standing rock still on the far side of the barge. But it wasn't just the figure that startled them. The condition of the person was like an unholy apparition from hell!

It was a woman, naked and bathed in crimson liquid. Her long, braided hair dripped with blood and carnage. A bejeweled necklace - ill-defined because of the blood - outlined her breasts. Her hands were held out to the side. A khopesh sickle sword was clenched in her right hand and - to everyone's indescribable horror - Lord Tao's bloody, mangled head was grasped firmly by his hair in her left hand.

With her head hanging down, she lifted her eyes: Bright green emeralds, burning hot. They bore into Pen-Nekhbet's soul with a sexual hunger that touched him with both revulsion and a savage desire.

Who was this woman?
Was this the princess?
Was she hurt?

The idea that the woman was the perpetrator was not the first thing that crossed Pen-Nekhbet's mind. She was coated in so much blood that it actually looked like she was part of the casualties. Oddly enough, what did cross his mind was that - even bloody with butchery - she was stunning. Eerily and horridly stunning. Her hypnotic stare caused everyone's reactions to slow. For what seemed like an eternity, no one moved.

And then slowly, she began a provocatively duplicitous stride towards the group. Her strangely sensual affectation was both morbid and exotic. So out of place for the context of what surrounded them, her entire aura was inexplicably erotic. The vision of her gruesome tantalization caused further hesitation among the warriors.

Casually tossing Tao's emancipated head at the archers dilatorily brought them to their senses. Too late, they let loose a volley of arrows.

The strange woman dodged and batted the flying arrows to the side with her khopesh as so much annoyance, suddenly breaking into a strident sprint towards the archers.

Pen-Nekhbet, momentarily taken by surprise quickly recovered as the screams of the archers echoed through the bowels of the ship. Unable to fully unsheathe their swords, they were left to the hellish woman's mercy - of which there was none. Twisting and turning between the four archers, the woman's blade silenced their cries with disemboweling slaughter. As a blur, the blood soaked woman quickly pushed through the archery contingent and converged on Admiral Apy with lightening speed. Twisting through the air, she brought her khopesh down in a sloping arc - slicing through the admiral's shoulder and deep into his chest cavity as his own unused sword clattered to the deck. Blood surged into the air with each desperate beat of Apy's heart, showering the gruesome angel of death.

Pen-Nekhbet was aghast. The woman actually seemed to delight in the arterial spray - moaning in joy from the admiral's blood that was raining down upon her.

But what seemed even more shocking was that Pen-Nekhbet thought he could sense the admiral sharing in her joy. As if Apy was delighted to be giving the angel of death pleasure at the horrifying way she took his life. The look of utter joy at giving the witch his life was written all over his face. Pen-Nekhbet was certain that Apy had purposely thrown his sword to the side as she brought his fate to him.

Pen-Nekhbet stumbled backwards in horror, instinctively grabbing Apy's khopesh from the deck. Unable to believe his eyes - yet knowing he would never be able to remove the gruesome vision - he saw the woman's tongue slither from between her teeth and lick the admiral's gore from her lips. Seductively. Her eyes closing as she delighted in the texture and the taste. Pulling the liquid into her mouth.

Suddenly, she kicked the admiral's depleted corpse free of her sword. Her penetrating stare fixated on Pen-Nekhbet as he stumbled backwards up the stairs. He tripped as he reached the top, his feet searching for a step that was no longer there. Careening recklessly onto the deck - his feet slipping in the varnish of blood - he searched for his footing. Luckily, some of the blood was beginning to dry and Pen-Nekhbet took quick advantage of the forming tacky surface.

Within two short leaps the angel of death mounted the stairs, her bare feet landing solidly onto the deck. She immediately launched into attack and Pen-Nekhbet whirled just in time to dodge a thrust from her wickedly curved blade. Knocking her sword aside, he followed through - spinning his body - the arc of his sword slicing through empty air. The woman anticipating the move had leaped out of the way. Following through, Pen-Nekhbet spun clear of a return slice from her sword.

Back and forth through the thickening fog, the battle raged. Each of them dodging, weaving and dancing together across the deck in an almost choreographed combination of attack and defense. Pen-Nekhbet could see a wicked smile appear on her focused face, her teeth a distinct contrast to the dark blood in which she was coated. It was a disturbing vision that caused a shiver to resonate deep within his soul.

But the exchange was also touching Pen-Nekhbet on a much deeper level.

Pen-Nekhbet was one of the best warriors in his class. Trained by his father in hand to hand combat - and with a number of weapons including the khopesh - he had won numerous competitions throughout Egypt. But this woman was like none he had ever encountered. The creepy smile and intensity of her green eyes - her entire naked body, covered in a ghoulish amount of blood and waste was distracting. Her skill with a khopesh sword was incredible. He knew she was just toying with him and for the first time, Pen-Nekhbet began to doubt his victory.

The woman attacked again, her blade narrowly missing Pen-Nekhbet's head. Through an extreme display of acrobatics - the like of which he had never witnessed before - Pen-Nekhbet felt the side of the woman's feet hit him hard in the chest. Stumbling backwards - his feet slipping in a pool of blood - he lost his grip on his sword and he heard it clang across the deck of the ship.

The woman somehow climbed up on him, worming her legs around his head like a snake. Suddenly - with a violent throw to the deck - he found himself lying on his back, pinned beneath her straddle - his breathing laboring. Stunned, he could only stare up into the woman's emerald eyes. Bright green jewels, glowing in the dim cast of the torchlight. An alarming amount of blood dripped from the woman's hair, splattering small droplets onto Pen-Nekhbet's chest and face - her smile contradictorily seductive. Her bright red tongue snaked from between her blood coated lips and leaning forward, she moaned sensually as she raked it across his mouth. Pen-Nekhbet could taste the carnage that coated her.

"We belong together, Pen-Nekhbet," she whispered seductively - a mixture of spittle and blood dripping from her lip.

It was all so odd - so horrid - yet, as Pen-Nekhbet stared into the angel of death's eyes, it was so inexplicably enticing. He now knew the joy that Apy felt when he gave his life to this enchantress. He too, wanted to say, *'yes'*. Wanted it badly. To give in to her desires. To please her. To have her.

Yes oh yes, he wanted her.

What was wrong with him?

With a supreme will, Pen-Nekhbet forced the spell of the angel of death from his mind. Replacing it instead with the image of Ipu - his beautiful nurse maiden that would be happily waiting for his return home. It was all he had, but it was enough.

"Who are you?" Pen-Nekhbet croaked.

The angel of death's provocative charm suddenly turned to rage - as if realizing that the spell she cast was ineffective and it inflamed her mania. The fire in her eyes rekindled and with a demonic cry, she raised her sword high.

Despite her incredible skill with a sword, her petite figure was no match for Pen-Nekhbet's strength and he reached his senses at the very last second. Pushing - lifting the woman above him and kicking hard - the woman flew into the air. Sailing into the fog-soaked darkness, he heard her body hit the river with a distant and distinct splash.

Grabbing his sword that lay nearby, Pen-Nekhbet breathlessly hurried to the side of the ship in an attempt to locate the woman as she struggled to the surface. He inexplicably wanted to save her. To recapture that erotic feeling again. To lose himself in the intensity of her stare.

But she never appeared and for Pen-Nekhbet, it was like a limb had been brutally removed. Bubbles floated to the surface, eventually subsiding until the water became still.

What was wrong with him?

A feeling of helplessness overcame him as he watched the Black River water swirl under the boat. He shook his head, trying to clear his mind from the sorcery the woman had held over him. His pulse throbbed heavy in his temples as he sank to his knees in stunned disbelief.

The *Wild Bull* was boarded and the captain of the guards was suddenly standing next to him. "Are you injured, my lord?"

Pen-Nekhbet figured that he looked as bad as the other casualties. He stood - breathing deep - trying to gather control. His mind was still reeling from the paradoxical situation that had occurred. The angel of death and the carnage she had produced was a strange dichotomy to the mesmerizing beauty she portrayed.

Who was the dark sorceress that had created such slaughter?
Where had she come from?

He suddenly spied something; a dark cloth lying in a heap on the blood soaked deck. Bending down, Pen-Nekhbet retrieved the item. It was the familiar cloak that had completely covered the person that had been haunting him since the *Heb Sed*.

Was the demon that had wreaked such damage the unseen princess, Sitkamose? And if so, how was he ever going to report her sorcery and bloodlust to the palace? The dark rumors that blossomed among the school children surrounding princess Sitkamose surfaced briefly.

A witch that delighted in the sexual perversions of the damned.

Pen-Nekhbet quickly shunned the thoughts in deference to his duty. Attempting to keep his voice from cracking as he brought his breathing under control - Pen-Nekhbet took charge, "Admiral Apy is dead, captain. Lord Tao and General Khafra are also dead. I have dispatched the perpetrator, but we need to secure this ship."

The captain of the guards snapped to attention and Pen-Nekhbet appreciated the respite to breathe another deep breath before continuing, "As of this moment, I - Pen-Nekhbet, royal herald from the house of Ah-Mose - am assuming command as the admiral in charge of this flotilla. Send a relief detail of row masters to this ship. We shall immediately resume a direct course for the port of Mennefer to ascertain our status and to secure the port. I want every hand armed and on alert."

"*Hoy!*" the captain of the guards shouted in acknowledgment, moving off with his men to carry out the orders he had been given.

Pen-Nekhbet stared out across the Black River his head still mired in a foggy state of disbelief. One question continuing to plague his mind,

Who was that goddess of death?

Thirty Eight

The Bay of Bengal; 2002

Jack Sterling's senses came alive as a low mist enveloped him. He squinted into the fog, but it was pitch black beyond. Something was alive out there, he knew it. He could sense it. He had felt it before. He could feel her approaching before he ever saw her. He could feel her heat. Smell her scent. Hear every breath she took. His every sense became engulfed with the burning sensuality she radiated. Animalistic, seductive. Even the way she walked as she came into view exuded intense sexuality.

Closer she came.

She was beautiful. Beautiful beyond reason. A goddess incarnate. Dressed simply in a smattering of a soft leather animal skin. Barely concealing her body and in fact, articulating her shape. Her feet were bare.

Her emerald green eyes held him spellbound with incredible bedroom intensity. Her hair fell across her shoulders in golden feathery locks as she focused on Sterling through several unruly strands. Her breathing was heavy, drenched in desire causing Sterling's own breaths to come in deep, powerful gasps. Her musky scent filled his nostrils.

His muddled mind told him that he had seen this woman before, hadn't he?

Yes! Of this, he was certain. But where and when, he could not place. Surely, if he had ever encountered such a seductive creature he would have remembered.

He searched his memory, yet she remained achingly out of reach. A mystery.

A beautiful, sensual mystery.

Closer still she came, stalking him as a predator stalked its prey. Perhaps she held realm merely in his dreams. But *this* was a dream, he *knew* this to be a dream. *A dream of dreams*. A phantom whisper of a memory or a desire unfulfilled. Yet this woman's essence captured him with such power that it seemed to pull the lust from his soul.

His own questions drifted absently and unanswered to the back of his mind until his own sexual desire dominated. Filling him until it became all he knew.

Closer still, she came.

He could feel his heart, pounding in his chest. His blood coursing through his veins and swelling him to aching proportions as she drifted seductively closer. Her lips parted slightly, her teeth subtlety bared, her expression enunciating her own aching need.

Closer.

"Jack," she whispered softly. So soft it was more felt than heard.

His mind was aflame. His soul was aflame. The need she initiated was becoming more than he could stand.

Cithimay!

Did he know her? God, why couldn't he remember? Yet why did he care?

"I want you, Jack," she pleaded. Her voice intoxicating. Her body melding into his, filling him with sensations of impossible pleasure.

He was possessed. Her words became music. Her every breath, a siren song that sang to his hunger. His emotions were running so high and deep, so powerful that he felt he would fall weeping at her feet.

'What the hell is wrong with me?' he said aloud. He could hear himself utter the words and it startled him.

Suddenly, he could hear shouting. Faint though - as if from a great distance. Yet so close. He could not place their location - these new voices - but he understood them. *"You must not give in! Fight it*!"

Her breath was on his neck, his mind was slipping.

Yes! Oh, God, Yes! He wanted this woman. He needed her. His need to be with her was all consuming. Drifting. Floating towards the beautiful woman, melting with her. Blending as one. He could feel her. Loving him. Devouring him. It was so good.

She was so good.

"I love you, Jack," she sang - her voice the song of a choir of angels. *"We belong together. I love you!"*

The other voices again - stronger, desperate, "Fight her. She must not win!"

He tried to ignore the voices. He knew what they wanted and he didn't want to listen. This phantom creature was strong and it felt so wonderful. So alluring. So captivating.

So familiar.

Demanding - She was demanding him to ignore the voices. Commanding his attention. "Come to me, Jack," her face now surrounded in angelic brilliance. He could not fight. Did not want to fight. He wanted this feeling. This woman.

This angel.

But the voices were insistent. Pleading, "Wake up, Captain. Don't let her win! She must not win!"

"*Doc?*" Sterling heard himself say - but he had no idea why. It was something that came to him. A familiar yet distant name.

Suddenly a single voice - as if the owner were hovering next to his ear. It was strong, calm, dignified, "Jasmine is in trouble Captain Sterling, please leave this beast and rescue her... *Now!*"

Sterling shook his head, struggling to clear his confusion. He knew this voice. He felt a trust. A familiarity but it seemed so long ago. Perhaps that was why the voice called him *captain*? He squeezed his eyes shut, "*No!*"

He felt the angel's grip slip just a bit. Her mind touched his again - filling him with that aching desire.

"Please, Jack," she sang in his head. "Come with me. Stay with me. *I love you, Jack!*"

"Who are you?" Sterling heard himself say. The question seemed immeasurably obtuse, but her spell seemed to weaken. Her entire mood shifted as she untangled herself from him. He felt her leaving his mind. The aching desire and sexual intensity she conveyed was rapidly turning to malevolence. He could feel within her an evil presence. An ancient wickedness, boiling to the surface.

In front of him, the mysterious and exquisite creature that had possessed him became something entirely different. Her once beautiful face became twisted with malice. The seductive arms that enveloped him in love and desire were now tentacles of an abomination. The sexual longing vanished into the mist as hatred prevailed.

A new emotion emerged within Sterling. An emotion he had long ago conquered and had even learned to use to his advantage. An emotion he had not felt in years.

Sterling was terrified.

And - as the once angelic woman let loose a scream that seemed to spring from the depths of hell itself, Sterling sprung from his bed - bathed in sweat, his heart pounding in his chest.

He opened his eyes to the gloom. The gentle rocking of the ship on the waves was disorienting and it took him a minute to remember where he was. The somber, disembodied voice from his dream echoed in his head, "*Jasmin is in trouble, Captain Sterling.*"

Jasmin.

He was alone in bed; Jasmin was no longer in the room. In the dim light Sterling found her *Shayla*.

Surely she had not been so foolish as to leave the cabin against her uncle's solemn warnings? Especially without her *Shayla*?

But that was exactly what had happened, Sterling realized as he searched for his pants. Pulling them over his hips with one hand as his other was opening the stateroom door, Sterling dashed into the hallway and found his way to the main deck.

The light was soft with the rising sun. The water and waves shimmered in the coming light. Sterling could feel the ocean chill on his bare skin, but his adrenaline was on overload as to pay it much mind. Immediately he saw a small grouping of men on the far side, huddled next to the port side railing. A body lay semi-visible between them; long dark hair splayed across the grimy deck of the old freighter.

"*Jasmin!*"

In defiance, the men refused to part as to allow Sterling through and he had to physically push them to the side. The looks on their faces were brimming with self-righteous hatred as he forced his way into the center. Jasmin lay unmoving. Blood pooling beneath her and spreading fast. Sterling had seen this kind of blood loss before and he knew before his knees dropped into the dark liquid that he was too late.

He cradled her head in his arms. Her eyes fluttered and opened. Recognition reigned and she smiled sweetly at the concerned face that looked back at her. "Jasmin," Sterling said softly - his heart breaking.

"Jack," she breathed - her smile wavering with shock. "I wanted to see the new sun-rise."

She coughed and the blood that pushed between her lips was bright red. Her eyes closed for a second, but opened again. She swallowed, hard. "Do not weep," she whispered. "You have freed me. It was my choice." Her breath was coming in shallow, blood lined spurts. The pool of blood underneath her was spreading rapidly and soaking through the thin fabric of his pants.

She touched his face and smiled, "I love you," her voice was barely a whisper.

Sterling was weeping, the tears running freely down his face. "I love you, Jasmin," he cried. And he did love this woman. She had willingly rescued him from certain death and it had cost her, her life.

Her smile widened at his words and immediately the light left her eyes.

She was gone.

Sterling held her. Burying his face next to hers, he cried. He cried for the little girl, helpless against the evil that took her parents and her innocence. He cried for the woman she became - a woman whose compassion was answered with only vitriolic ignorance. And he cried in anger against the cruelty and the injustice spreading across the world and the people who allowed it to thrive.

The men were still gathered around him. A voice from the crowd boldly stated in Arabic, "She was a disgrace to Islam!"

Unfortunately for the crew of the freighter, it was the wrong thing to say to Jack Sterling. The highly trained, elite fighting force of one was in no mood to be lectured to by a primitive thug. His grief turned to anger and then cascaded beyond.

Jack Sterling was pissed!

Laying Jasmin's head gently to the deck, Sterling stood and faced the crew that had gathered. Ten men who now foolishly thought that strength lay in their numbers. Ten men whose faces portrayed an indifferent sanctimony that only fueled Sterling's rage. He let his gaze drift to each mans eyes as his brain processed how the next few seconds would proceed.

It was not going to be a matter of how many men would now die; it was only a matter of who would be first.

Thirty Nine

Boston, Massachusetts; Present Day

Stephen Andrews led Lownsbury into the basement of the Otis mansion where museum offices occupied most of the space. As he walked he spoke of the incredible discovery of the box.

"The box is in surprisingly good condition. Although the leather is worn and the embroidered hieroglyphics are almost illegible to the naked eye, the wood framing is in remarkably fine shape."

Lownsbury was dejected. His enthusiasm had evaporated when he learned of the confiscation of the gun by the government. The box alone would have - at one time - elicited a singular excitement in him for the historical significance that it held. Now it seemed a meaningless vessel; a novelty that held little importance except for the proof it offered that it had indeed, belonged to Samuel Parris.

He began to imagine how he could make contact with his team back in Colorado. He looked at his watch. They were still a good three weeks away from the initial test run of *The Machine*. By now his Colorado self would have informed them of the possibilities of future contact. How could he have allowed his time phone to have become so blithely destroyed? Lownsbury suddenly felt like he was wasting his time. He would need to be quick in making sure that this was indeed the Reverend Parris's box.

Andrews was still droning on about the box as they navigated through the basement. His voice remained all but unheard as Lownsbury blindly followed him through a small anteroom into a larger room beyond; the storage and restoration chamber. Lownsbury's mind was elsewhere as Andrews unlocked a closet door - stepped inside - and retrieved a large package.

When Andrews reappeared with a large, burlap-covered item, Lownsbury's excitement returned and he found himself unable to breathe. Andrews pulled the box free of the burlap bag and placed it on a low workshop table.

Lownsbury was awestruck. He had not realized how seeing this box again would allow so much emotion to resurface. It had only been a few days ago when he had last laid eyes on the pristine version of the chest and at that time, he had barely given it a glance.

At Andrews's behest, Lownsbury donned a pair of surgical gloves before he ran his fingers along the box's cracked and aged surface. Tracing the outline of each faded image, he remembered how the box once looked sitting atop a table inside the Parris's residence in Salem Village. He remembered his hasty foray into the parlor to retrieve what he could of the contents it once held. Now it seemed so much a surreal piece of antiquity.

"It used to be red," he heard himself say as he ran his fingers along the rim.

A doorbell chime was heard somewhere in the old mansion and it brought Lownsbury out of his reverie. "May I open it?" He asked - his excitement peaking.

"Oh, please do," Andrews responded - making his way around the table.

The doorbell chime sounded again and Andrews looked at his watch. "My next appointment is early. Please excuse me, professor."

Turning - just before leaving the room - Andrews smiled, "If you're looking to help settle the dispute concerning authenticity, the other items in that box are just as provocative as the gun. I will return momentarily."

Lownsbury returned his attention to the box as Stephen Andrews made his way back to the main level. He could hear his heavy footsteps crossing through the drawing room on his way to the foyer.

Lownsbury gently lifted the lid on the ancient container. Inside were three little bundles of wrapped parchment. Their surfaces were yellowed with age; frail and brittle. Lownsbury gently lifted one of the bundles out of the box and gingerly pulled at the edges. The disappointment he felt upon learning of the confiscation of the ancient Glock vanished as he laid eyes on what was wrapped within the folds of the ancient paper.

Lownsbury could hear the voices upstairs as Andrews greeted his scheduled caller - the two were exchanging pleasantries. He ignored the sound of the door closing and two sets of footsteps making their way back across the foyer towards the basement entrance. His attention was instead focused on the contents of the first bundle. There could be no doubt that this three hundred year old box once belonged to Samuel Parris as he held - once again - the ragged remains of his old pipe. It had not survived the ravages of time as the rest of the box had and Lownsbury reasoned that someone - perhaps Parris himself - had used the pipe for the remainder of their lives. There was no mistaking however, that the pipe was not a seventeenth century model.

Stephen Andrews and the newcomer could still be heard on the floor above - their voices muffled through the flooring as Lownsbury pulled the second paper wrapped bundle from the interior of the box and began to gently peel back the folds. What lay within removed all thought of preserving the wrapper and Lownsbury tore into the delicate paper.

His heart was racing; his breathing became deep and labored as he pulled a cell phone screen from the second time phone that had been left behind in Salem from the folds of the ancient paper.

Could it be?

Could it still work after all this time?

The screen appeared to be in near perfect shape. A few rust marks could be seen on some of the components but all in all, it seemed intact. He remembered he still had the pieces of his own disassembled phone in his jacket pocket and his path became clear. He could almost feel his salvation at hand.

The voices upstairs were still muddled. Stephen Andrews and his guest had paused in the hallway and he could hear Andrews talking to the newcomer about some display or another. There was a laugh, a scrape across the floor and then a voice that froze Lownsbury's blood. Any elation he had once had over finding parts to repair his time phone, vanished.

It was a single word - spoken with such clarity and cadence that there could be no mistake as to who the newcomer was.

"Excellent!"

The sound reverberated through the floor and walls of the large mansion and seemed to surround Lownsbury in the tiny storage room deep in the basement.

Schulte!

Lownsbury's fingers found new life. Pulling pieces from his coat pocket, he arranged them across the workbench. Small meshes of wires and other components were plugged and unplugged as he struggled to get the new found screen attached to his current phone. He didn't know if the screen would work or not - but it was all he had.

He heard a thump and a loud crash; something heavy hit the floor upstairs. It sounded as if Andrews was in trouble. Lownsbury resisted the urge to run to his aid. The need to get the phone working dominated his thoughts. The workroom in the basement was cool but beads of sweat began to run down the bridge of his nose. At the tip of his nose, a drop dangled for a brief second. Lownsbury roughly wiped it away. Fear was gripping him and he struggled to remain calm - control his breathing.

He could hear the footsteps again - only one set this time - slowly advancing through the rooms of the mansion. The sound of the footfalls purposeful and methodical.

Unnerving.

Like a jigsaw puzzle he pressed on, placing the small bits of plastic in the slots in which they would fit. The adhesive used in the manufacture of the aged cell phone screen was useless and Lownsbury struggled to keep the arranged pieces intact.

William had created the phones by cannibalizing older, store bought units and adjusting them to operate exclusively with *The Machine*. Lownsbury had helped Will disassemble and re-assemble each of these phones components and he was now very grateful for that experience.

Schulte began to whistle a tune. Unfamiliar, indistinct yet obscenely condescending. Lownsbury gambled that Schulte was aware of his presence. He could imagine the conversation that had taken place with Andrews when Schulte had arrived:

The greeting; small talk; an offering of flattery from and to each of them and finally, the request to see the box. The explanation that Professor Larimer Lownsbury had also arrived and was - even now - perusing the contents of the box in the basement. Further small talk had ensued and when Schulte saw his opportunity for attack, he had taken it - neutralizing Andrews. To what degree, Lownsbury could only guess.

The sounds above had stopped and the echoes of footfalls down the staircase had begun. Slow, determined. The whistling, maddeningly persistent.

Almost there!

Lownsbury pushed the phone parts together, but he still had no screws in which to keep the phone intact. He grabbed the remaining paper wrapped bundle from inside the box and stuffed it into his coat pocket.

The echoing reverberations of Schulte's footsteps suddenly ceased. Lownsbury's breath caught. The abrupt silence became more unsettling than the sounds of Schulte's advancement; like the cessation of drum beats prior to an imminent savage attack.

Lownsbury's senses heightened, he instinctively raised his eyes. The rooms were clear.

He didn't know if the aged cell phone screen would work or not, but there was no time to worry about it now. It was do or die. Lownsbury glanced down, pressed the power button and immediately brought his line of sight back to the doorway and the outer room and beyond.

Schulte was standing right in front of him - just on the other side of the workbench!

"*Sweet Jesus!*" He exclaimed stumbling backwards.

The Senator's miraculous appearance had taken Lownsbury entirely by surprise. His glance to his phone had been so brief that there was no natural manner in which the man could have navigated the length of the two rooms with such speed.

"Good evening Professor," Schulte's smile was gracious - but his eyes bristled with a level of malevolence. "*How fortuitous.*"

ᶠorty

JAG Headquarters, Washington D.C.; 2002

Lieutenant General Robert Schneider's mind drifted. Thoughts of retirement once again flickered through his head as he settled back into his office chair. The soft, supple leather conveyed the essence of comfort. But it did little to settle the growing irritation he had been experiencing as of late. Perhaps his wife was right. Perhaps he was turning into a curmudgeon. Just like his father. But *goddamnit*, there were just certain things that pissed him off!

Ok, there were a *lot* of things that pissed him off.

For instance, take this damn office!

His office was more lavish than he cared for. It represented the epitome of a certain style and flair that would fit well within the pages of a *Forbes 500* magazine. And although the opulence would have come to be something expected among many Americans that had reached his station, Schneider's attitude was becoming more and more one of minimization. He was beginning to miss the simpler things in life: Sitting on a log in front of a fire - surrounded by the peace and quiet of a forest; pulling a large trout from the hellacious pull of a rushing river. Hell, just pissing behind a tree was becoming one of his more enticing life desires.

He let loose a weary sigh. Retirement seemed to be a frequently occurring idea with each new passing year and the exponentially growing bureaucracy he was forced to deal with every day only seemed to reinforce that dream. Every new batch of congressmen brought with them more of the same old, *'new ideas'*. More of the same old, *'new pet projects'*. And a perpetually increasing gaggle of lawyers with their swelling reams of paperwork.

Lawyers and paperwork. Paperwork and lawyers. The two were irrevocably linked. You just couldn't have one without the other. And if there was one thing General Schneider knew about himself, it was his hatred for paperwork. There were times that he regretted ever becoming a lawyer just because of the paperwork it required.

He sighed; maybe he *was* turning into a curmudgeon. Perhaps he should take his wife's advice and stop looking at the negatives in life and make an effort to try to see the positives. But with all the senseless violence that seemed to be bubbling around him, it was hard to find optimism anywhere... anymore. He was a lawyer. And he was a good one. And he still had his dignity and a sense of humility. He had worked hard his whole life to become appointed without having to sell his soul by pursuing the election route. Appointed lawyers were bad enough - he had long ago decided - but the elected lawyers were the worst of all. Elections seemed to be the magic ingredient that filled every bureaucrat with blood-sucking delusions of nobility.

As the appointed commander at the District of Columbia's Judge Advocate General's office, Lieutenant General Schneider considered lawyers to be the most dangerous threat to the American way of life. Terrorists were nothing compared to the insidious back handed tactics of lawyers. Get a group of them together with a powerful insurance lobby and the damage they could wreak was legion.

Like this new Homeland Security Department that was being touted. *Oh, and there was something else!*

The new Homeland Security Department - Christ, if the people only knew. And know they eventually would. And thus, would begin the legal battles. Long, drawn out, very expensive court decisions surrounding every nuance that arose through the cracks of each phrase, each word and every comment of the law. And of course, you can't have an enormous legal battle without the taxpayers covering the massive legal bills.

But in the end, it was all the same. All of it designed as yet another excuse to steal one more dollar from the taxpayer's wallet. Another excuse to pull apart a few more freedoms. Another reason to put one more *goddamn* lawyer into a cushy government position. And in return, drown everyone in countless reams of more fucking paperwork!

Christ, there he went again.

'Curmudgeon Bob' and his inner-fucking diatribe!

He breathed so hard he nearly groaned as he looked at the file of his latest case. Another prime example of an entire nation's abandonment of common sense. A young private named Baker that had killed an Afghani terrorist without having first been fired upon. He threw the file back down on his desk.

"*Christ! What the hell was this country coming too*?" he muttered out loud. One less piece of human debris in the world and we spend time prosecuting our own. "*The man should be given a fucking medal*!" He yelled to his empty office.

He rubbed his eyes as he settled back into his office chair. *Son of a bitch*! It was only eleven a.m. and he already needed a drink.

Schneider glanced up to his television. A pretty, young Fox News reporter was narrating a breaking story and the headline had caught his eye. God knew he needed a distraction. He absent mindedly reached for the remote and turned up the volume:

"... and we are warning viewers that some of these images may be graphic," the reporter explained in a lilting feminine voice.

The picture on the screen changed to an overhead angle of a medium sized freighter, lodged on a shallow reef. The ship was tilting at a sickening angle. Several of the larger cargo containers had fallen from the deck and could be seen settling into the shallow waters.

The reporter continued, "A Pakistani freighter - the PFS Karachi - was in route to the Hawaiian Islands, when it ran aground on a reef in the Malacca Strait - just outside of Singapore. The captain was apparently the sole survivor aboard the vessel. He described a tale of being boarded by an American assassin who decimated his entire crew and his family, before mysteriously disappearing. And although the captain was quickly sequestered, it is confirmed that sixteen members of his crew - including one woman whose identity is still unknown - were killed in what can only be described as a vicious and brutal assault."

The picture on the screen changed. The deck of the ship was visible showing several bodies dangling from the railings as they hung out over the breaking waters. The otherwise white rails were colored in a deep crimson.

"The surviving captain claims that he had unintentionally grounded the ship in an attempt to pilot the vessel - single handedly - through the narrow strait. He further alleged that he was forced into the Singapore shipping lanes by the person or persons responsible and that the perpetrators disappeared shortly before his ship ran aground.

"Singapore authorities however, cannot confirm this claim.

"Investigation of the incident is ongoing but the early indications are that they believe the captain may have suffered from a nervous breakdown. A source at the scene told us that the amount of death and damage inflicted suggests that one man - acting alone - is a highly improbable scenario. And that this was - more likely than not - a concerted effort.

"The State Department is rejecting the captain's assertions that this was an American attack stating that no operation of any military personnel was sanctioned and that the attack is likely the actions of pirates known to troll the area - or a possible *'friendly fire'* terrorist attack.

"Muslim leaders throughout the Middle East are decrying the assault however, stating that the strike on the civilian freighter is merely unjustified retribution for the Nine Eleven attack that occurred in New York nearly a year ago and that the State Department's comments are incendiary und unprovoked.

"Again, if you are just tuning in, a civilian Pakistani freighter ran aground late last night..."

Schneider punched a button on his remote, silencing the television. *'Wonderful,'* he thought to himself. This will undoubtedly cause some bureaucrat to respond with more fucking paperwork. He closed his eyes and put his head in his hands. God, a campfire would smell good right about now!

Retirement again crossed Schneider's mind, but these thoughts were cut short as his personal cell phone vibrated inside his pocket. The number was unknown to anyone outside of his personal circle. *'Here we go,'* he thought to himself - instinctively standing as he punched the answer button - *'The first of the fallout.'*

"Hi Bob, its Jack," a familiar - yet unexpected voice from the grave echoed through his phone.

Schneider dropped back into his chair. "Jack? Sterling? What the hell? Good lord man! It has been almost three months since anyone has heard from you. Where the fuck have you been?"

"I need some help."

"No shit, you need help! Everyone on the hill has heard about the shit that went down at Saddam's palace. Someone high up wants to bring the hammer down on you - *hard*!" Schneider's voice was laced with a mixture of emotions.

A brief silence and then Schneider's voice came back, uneasy - broken with concern, "Jesus, Jack! You had all of us worried! What the fuck happened?!"

"Listen, Bob. What went down is not what you might think. We were set up. My team was sent in there as sacrificial lambs. There are some high level players on our side of the fence that are up to their necks in shit and I plan on making them eat some of it."

"Wait a minute Jack," Schneider said - shaking his head in confusion. "Slow down. What are you saying?"

"I'm saying, I need to be brought in and debriefed. I need to testify to congress on what I witnessed in Iraq and I need you to get me in there." Sterling's voice lowered, "Bob, this goes deep. Bone deep. This shit involves some high ranking players."

"You might want to tread carefully around that, Jack. You just can't waltz into congress making accusations." Schneider sighed - a thought occurring to him, "Wait a minute, who the fuck are we talking about anyways?"

"Senator Ted Schulte. He was in Iraq, Bob. My memory suddenly became very clear with this. He was there with Saddam and Osama and from everything I heard, he was the mastermind behind Nine Eleven. He had my entire team killed to create an international incident to keep the United States out of Iraq. I barely made it out alive."

Schneider let out a long breath, "Hold on a second, Jack." He put the phone down and pulled a bottle of *'Ol' Granddad'* and a glass from his desk. He poured himself a double, neat - repeat.

Perhaps eleven a.m. was a good time to start drinking.

'Curmudgeon Bob,' He whispered quietly to himself. He had to admit, he was getting used to the name.

Schneider picked the phone back up and put it to his ear. "You said your memory is clear?" - Shaking his head - "That's a stiff fucking charge, Jack!" - exhaling heavily - "You might want to rethink that position. Nobody gets anywhere trying to nail a senior senator to the wall. And Schulte is about as senior as it gets."

"This is some serious shit, Bob."

"No fucking kidding this is serious shit, Jack!" Schneider yelled - his anger suddenly peaking. "Insubordination, desertion, murder of Iraqi civilians! Jesus Christ, you can forget your Major's pension! I'll be fucking lucky to get your sentence commuted to death for treason! By the way, was that you on that goddamn Pakistani boat? *Goddamnit*, it was, wasn't it?! And then you just traipse back in here? *Fuck me, Jack!*"

A long semi-silence opened up between them as Schneider vented his anger between drawn out breaths infused with long, unilateral bouts of cursing. Sterling even thought he heard him kicking something - perhaps a trashcan. But finally, his swearing devolved into low guttural grunting. Eventually, he became coherent. "Ok. Let's pretend that what you told me is even remotely true," - now with a slight sniffle - "That Senator Schulte is a traitor - a bad guy - blah, blah, blah. Let me tell you what *you* will be facing, Jack:

"First of all it will take years of legal mumbo jumbo to even get anywhere near him. His lawyers - at the taxpayer's expense - mind you - will bog you down in so much paperwork, it would take a bulldozer to unbury you. His cronies will surround him, they will protect him and they will inundate the media with hit pieces on you *and* anyone you care about. By the time you get your day in court, you and everyone you know will become pariahs of the community. You will be broke. You will be shamed. You will be dishonorably discharged. And - to top it all off - by the time you see an actual judge, the matter will be so much a distant memory that the public won't even care about it - or you - anymore.

"And even after all that, Jack. Let's say you win. Let's say you can draw yourself a deep, self-satisfied breath and pat yourself on the goddamn back for winning one in the name of truth, justice and American goddamn way. After you look out over the destruction and the misery and the lives that have been torn apart in the wake of your principled quest, what the fuck do you think *his* punishment will be? Really? This is a pipe dream Jack! No! I *will* bring you in. You *will* turn yourself in and we *will* go to congress with contrition and remorse. *Not* with allegations."

The encroaching silence was punctuated only by the heavy breathing from both ends. Sterling was used to his friend ranting and raving about one thing or another. Odd as it had seemed to everyone, it had become a cornerstone of their friendship. Yet the silence suddenly became too long.

"What the fuck do you expect, Jack?" Schneider said - breaking the unnerving silence. "I've always told you, we don't get to pick winners and losers, Major. Come in, so we can deal with this."

Sterling finally replied, "If I can't find justice for this piece of shit through you, then I will search for it myself."

The line suddenly went dead, leaving Schneider enveloped in disquieting silence.

forty One

Boston, Massachusetts; Present Day

Time seemed to be out of cadence. There was nothing definitive Lownsbury could determine with that assessment, but everything just seemed - out of sync. Disorienting. And - to put it simply - terrifying. His hands were shaking, his palms were sweaty. He managed to control his breathing long enough to ask, "What have you done with Mr. Andrews?"

Schulte lifted his eyebrows, genuinely confused, "I am sorry, Professor. To whom are you referring?"

"The caretaker of this museum, what have you done with him?" He said louder - trying keep his voice from cracking.

Schulte put a finger to his chin, "Oh, good heavens Professor, I'd nearly forgotten." Then he smiled, "You need not worry about Mr. Andrews, he will not be interrupting us."

"*What have you done with him*?" Lownsbury insisted - the pitch of his voice increasing in tandem to his fear.

Schulte's eyes narrowed and he took a menacing step forward, "Do you really want to know the details?" - A slight pause - "Professor?"

Lownsbury swallowed hard. Schulte's previously unassuming persona was forfeit. It was now as if the whole universe expanded and contracted with every breath the senator took.

Terrifying!

In one swift move, Lownsbury managed to pull his .38 revolver from the pocket of his coat and began firing. Screaming. His emotions were on overload and he was panicked. He had only five shots in the small snub nose and he went through every one until the hammer had only expended casings to strike. The gun clicked in relative silence to the rapid explosions that had so recently filled the tiny, basement room.

Lownsbury was stunned. None of the rounds had found their target. Sweat had been pouring into his eyes - clouding his vision - but the imagery still seemed so surreal. It had appeared that Schulte had shimmered into near transparency throughout the pulse pounding gun fire, finally solidifying as the pistol's chamber made its full revolution. It had appeared that the senator had not so much as flinched during the gun play - the same cock-sure smile and damnable tilt of his head, only seemed to enunciate the futility of the Professor's efforts.

Lownsbury continued to hold the useless pistol at the senator as his panicked mind attempted to come to grips with his reality. His ears were ringing and he was still sweating profusely.

Schulte - ignoring the murderous intent on his life as if it were a simple, everyday occurrence - turned his head slowly and looked at the Parris box. The lid was still open. He brought his eyes back to Lownsbury. His smile softened - genuine this time, "I believe my most pressing question has been answered, wouldn't you say, Professor?"

Lownsbury's terror was calming, becoming overshadowed with dejection. Schulte had obviously figured out where and when Samantha was. The gun he continued to hold seemed so petty. Useless. There was now nothing that anyone could do to stop the son of a bitch.

"I have little time at the moment Professor," - Schulte lifted his chin - "I will soon need to rush to my daughters aid - as you can imagine. But I also do not wish to be rude. There is still so much we need to discuss."

Schulte looked to the Parris box again. He chuckled slightly in reminiscence, "Although a bit out of place, I am suddenly reminded of one of my favorite tales," - side-saddling against the worktable as he casually fingered the remaining items inside the antique chest - "An ancient story from the days of Solomon. Retold many times through the ages, but a recent recantation I find so apt for our circumstances."

Schulte smiled with his trademark disarming tilt of his head as he began his story, "It seems there was once a merchant in Baghdad, who had sent his servant to the local market for provisions. The man was gone only a short while, unexpectedly arriving back empty handed and quite shaken.

"This servant relayed a story to his master that - while he was at the marketplace, he had come upon a woman. A woman that he had immediately recognized..." Schulte turned his head to Lownsbury and dramatically deepened his voice, "...*as Death.*"

Schulte's subtle pause and enunciation of the word - although made with a trace of humor - caused a shiver to run through Lownsbury.

Schulte continued with returned good humor, "The servant stated that the woman had made a threatening gesture, scaring the hell out of him. Well, after telling his master this story of the strange woman, the servant then begged him to borrow a horse so that he may flee Baghdad. His plan was to travel to the town of Samarra - a good distance away - where he believed that *Death* would not find him."

Lowering his voice - he leaned forward, "Well, the merchant allowed his servant the use of one of the horses and the frightened young man left at great speed for Samarra, certain of finding safety there. The merchant in turn, traveled to the marketplace himself to make up for the delinquency of his servant." - Schulte leaned back and sniffed - "A more tolerant disposition for such blatant insubordination than I would have had - I assure you."

Schulte picked up the ruined remains of Lownsbury's pipe stem with a small level of fascination and then dropped it back to the table in obvious disgust - shaking his head in subtle disbelief. "But I digress," he said - removing his handkerchief from his suit coat and wiping his fingers.

Clearing his throat - he resumed the story, "Wandering through the marketplace, the merchant stumbled upon the woman his servant had seen and he begins to understand his servant's fright. The woman was in fact - *Death.* Curious, the merchant approached her to ask why she made threatening gestures to his servant - scaring him so?

"Upon which she answered - 'I made no threatening gesture, sir. I was merely surprised to see him in Baghdad - *for I have an appointment with him tonight in Samarra.*'"

Schulte cast his eyes to the ceiling - his smile broadening. "I find that story simply the absolute epitome of irony - don't you professor?"

The unanswered question hung awkwardly in the now silent room.

"As Solomon himself would say: '*A man's feet are responsible for him, for they take him where he is wanted.*' And here I find you."

Schulte sighed as he refocused - standing, "I had recruited you as my soldier, Professor. I am keenly disappointed that we should be at odds."

"I am not your soldier," Lownsbury responded - confused. His attention diverted by a small stab of light that suddenly appeared in his hands.

The time phone!

Schulte let his eyes drift to the phone clutched tightly in Lownsbury's sweaty grip.

His terror waning, Lownsbury's thumb hovered over the keypad of the phone - poised to push a button. His logical mind however, was clawing its way to the surface as he began to realize the unique opportunity of information that could be gleaned from the senator. Questions that still demanded answers.

Schulte suddenly leaned across the table towards Lownsbury. As if reading his mind - he said, "Before we take our leave from one another Professor, I would like for you to consider your destination. Your presence here to retrieve this box makes it abundantly clear where my daughter is. I would suggest you waste no more energy towards those efforts. I shall stress that there is nothing you or anyone else can do."

Schulte smiled and righted himself, "No. I instead urge you now to consider your destiny." His eyes narrowed - his voice dropping, "Might I suggest that you use your time wisely in the pursuit of information. My goal professor is the pursuit of history. A goal you can surely appreciate and one in which I desperately need your help. What I seek is an artifact. As ancient as mankind. An artifact that was lost to the sands of time, yet still exists within the subconscious memory of all humans. An artifact that will end all sickness and hunger. It will bring mankind together with a purpose. A gift from the God of gods and one that should not be squandered. Never has the artifact been more needed than today. Together, we can bring mankind peace and prosperity."

Lownsbury shook his head - his thumb still poised, "An old pipe dream senator. A wild goose chase that serves nothing more than to ensure you power."

Schulte smiled, "There is still so much you do not know, professor. I only ask that you do not demonize that which you do not yet understand. Learn what you can before you condemn me." He leaned in closer - his voice a harsh whisper, "Remember professor, A wise man will allow faith to be a guiding principle, if not done so blindly. Blind faith - often times - is the epithet of wanton ignorance."

Leaning closer to Lownsbury - Schulte suddenly closed his eyes and inhaled deeply. A look of joy appearing. "I did not realize that the heavenly aroma of the *Velatova* lingers upon you. It has been years since

I have smelled that wonderful bouquet." He inhaled deeply again, "Ah, but I envy you."

Lownsbury frowned - confused.

Schulte opened his eyes, "Oh, but you likely do not remember. A somewhat bothersome side effect. *Velatova* is a long extinct flower, professor. Used by my people to anesthetize, but the recipient of the drug would often forget the experience. My guess is you were likely taken for inoculations." - Lifting his eyebrows - "Mother does like to keep tabs on the Elders - and even potential Elders - traipsing through time. She likes to keep history's plagues to a minimum if she can." He waved his hand in the air - smiling, *"Mothers,"* he said - as if offering some dismissive explanation.

Snapshots of memory invaded Lownsbury's mind. Vague snapshots. Like lingering remnants of a long forgotten dream.

Ambrosia.

Evalana!

Finally - "Remember: Your destiny awaits. As do I. Until next time, professor?" Schulte turned and began to walk back through the ante-chamber door. But as Lownsbury stared after him, he seemed to shimmer in the dim light of the basement - vanishing into thin air.

It all seemed impossible.

Lownsbury ran his fingers through the stubble of hair on his head - trying to relax his shaking hands. He shook his head in disbelief.

He stood for a long moment deciding his next move. He now realized his attempt at retrieving the gun from Reverend Parris's box had been an exercise in futility. He further realized that since Schulte had not returned, he had certainly found his daughter.

Lownsbury felt beaten. There did not seem to be any way to overcome the man.

No, not a man - more a demon from the pits of hell. He must be. His uncanny ability at time travel was unbelievable. Lownsbury thought that if *he* were having this much difficulty at trying to stay ahead of Schulte, the rest of his team was surely experiencing the same thing. They had underestimated the evil senator at every turn.

Evil?

Lownsbury realized he now had a trace of doubt in this regard.

Lownsbury closed his eyes in thought. What he needed was to find out more about Senator Theodore Godescalcus Schulte. He was consistently underestimating the man. He needed to find some method of getting on top. Schulte was right; he needed information.

And Lownsbury knew just the place.

Adjusting the time and geographic coordinates, he purposefully - yet mildly - hyperventilated in preparation. His determination steeled - his stance resolute. It was time to find out who - or what - this son of a bitch was.

Epilogue

Salem Village, Massachusetts; Spring, 1692

Trapped in a dingy, fetid cell in 17th century Massachusetts, Samantha Moon lay upon the chilled, damp earth - a mere scattering of straw the only barrier between her and the dirt.

A centipede slithered its way between a few withered stalks of straw and Samantha's splayed fingers. She shivered as icy tentacles of numbing pain lanced through her body causing the startled centipede to hasten its pace across the dusty soil - slithering evasively to and fro in its attempt to escape.

It had been several weeks since Larimer Lownsbury had escaped Salem Village - abandoning her to her horrible fate. Fall was fast approaching as summer neared its end and she cringed at the thought of spending another New England winter in this cell.

As fast as her deterioration was occurring however, she doubted she would see little more of the sweltering, New England summer heat much less its icy touch of winter. The onset of her deterioration and the rapidity of her decline had been staggering. The effects of being separated from her father were now so devastating, that she had been unable to move from the floor since yesterday. Incapable of even eating or using her waste bucket - she could feel her organs liquefying and her muscles withering. The effort it took to even open her eyes proved unbearable.

She looked at her hands as they lay in the dirt - wasted and shrunken. Her skin had become the color of ripened bananas - blackening from extreme age. A tear drifted down her dark, sunken cheek, evaporating into the dirt. "Please, no!" she wept - her voice barely above a whisper.

She could sense others in the cramped cell with her, though she could no longer see them. These were women whom she had publicly accused of witchcraft. Women whose families had stood in the way of Magistrate John Hathorne's plans for capturing their land and the coal buried beneath it. Women that would likely suffer certain death because Samantha had helped Hathorne eradicate them with her damning testimonies of bewitchment. Those very women were now witnessing their retribution in a terrifying and ghastly manner as their accuser withered into a blackened, shrunken husk. They remained huddled in their corner, conversing in hushed whispers as they watched her writhe in silent agony. She heard a voice in the darkness whisper, *The devil now come for ye!*"

To Samantha, it couldn't happen soon enough.

Samantha Moon drifted in and out of consciousness as visions of her own retribution danced through what was left of her mind. Larimer Lownsbury occupied most of those hazy thoughts - the son of a bitch that had left her there to suffer alone in the dark of this cold dungeon. It seemed impossible that the fool had deceived her so well.

Perhaps not so impossible, she considered. Her mental acuity was already being affected when Lownsbury had teamed with the women in the adjoining cell to achieve his own escape. Having the women hold her in place as he vanished into time had been a stroke of genius on his part, she had to admit.

But for her not to have realized that the pompous, narcissistic Magistrate Hathorne would have double crossed her as well was a true testament to her mental corrosion. She was rapidly losing her mind. At the onset of her plague, Hathorne had deserted her just as Lownsbury had - casting her aside as so much trash. It was at this point, that Samantha began to publicly recant her earlier assertions of the townswomen's satanic tendencies. With no hope of ever seeing Hathorne again in his chambers, she was hoping her retraction and accusations of corruption would see the good magistrate locked down here in a cell with her. Down here in the damp, darkness where she would be able to dish out her own form of justice.

But even this was not to be. The other town magistrates had looked the other way to Hathorne's improprieties and now she was far too advanced in her atrophy to even consider such actions. All she could do now was lay fetal on the floor as decay ran unmercifully through her body.

A spasm blasted through her arm causing her to draw it up. The fingers on her left hand curled into a grotesque claw as tendons splintered away from bones. Samantha screamed in agony, but only a harsh whisper escaped her desiccated lips.

The other women - watching the unholy drama unfolding before them - shrieked in terror. Clawing at each other, they raced to the cell door - crying desperately for anyone within earshot.

The pain subsided and Samantha dropped her head to the straw, weeping openly in helpless agony. Oh, God how she wished for death! She longed for anything that could bring an end to this unbearable suffering.

She had experienced this before when her father had been exiled, so very long ago. She had lost count of the number of years it had been, but the pain it caused was forever a lingering memory. Even now - as her curse resurrected itself in this godless hole of hell - she could recall the inconceivable anguish that still awaited her.

As the other of those accused settled along the cell's perimeter and quieted into hushed prayers, Samantha found herself joining them. Silently, she prayed to God for the end of this terrible torment. Yet, she knew her own prayer for the sweet release of death would go unanswered. She would linger in and out of consciousness, tortured in agony until her brain would become unable to function. Eventually, the unending anguish would become all that she would know. She mercifully closed her eyes, awaiting the next grinding spasm that would continue to pull her body slowly apart.

Yet, something entirely different happened.

A warming sensation arose within her chest; a promising spark that slowly began to flicker just beneath her sternum. Ever brighter it burned with the omnipresent glow of deliverance. Samantha opened her eyes in hope.

Could it be?

Yes!

She pushed past her pain and smiled in the gloom of the dwindling light.

A prayer answered, but it wouldn't be the release of death that freed her.

No.

The warmth that now fed her and spread through her body was an answer to another prayer. Her plea for salvation was the prayer that would be answered today. She could feel *Him* coming. *He* was here! *He* was in Salem, and *He* had come for her!

His presence was the release from this pain she had longed for.

As the encroaching warmth spread through her with each closing step her father took, she lost consciousness for the final time. Blackness found her. Enveloped her. Pulled her into nothingness. And as she sank into that wonderful, black abyss, three names played over and over through her mind. Three adversaries that had unexpectedly won a small battle, but would soon find out that the war was far from over.

Encore

London, England: Whitechapel; August 31 1888, 3:30 am.

The arrival into the early morning hours was cold and very wet - as most autumn evenings were in London. The moon was well into a waning crescent phase but the woman that was stumbling along Buck's Row in Whitechapel, likely couldn't have seen it even if the sky was clear. She was hopelessly drunk and was having difficulty in keeping her footsteps in view, much less what lay above in the dreary, cloud filled sky.

Being in search of a man that could keep her pub crawl going, Mary Nichols - or *Polly*, as her friends called her - stumbled down Buck's Row towards the Roebuck pub house at the corner of Brady Street - hoping she could get a pint in exchange for a quick shagging. She had already entertained a number of men in the last couple of hours with the purpose of paying for her doss, but had chosen drink instead of a bed each time. This deep into her drunk, a bed was now no longer even a consideration.

Looking up from her shoes - her head and mind barely able to maintain - she made out the figure of a young woman making her way to intercept. She was dressed very well for being on Bucks Row; a hooded cloak partially concealing her features - but not hiding so much that her exquisite details could be mistaken.

Polly smiled as the woman drew near. "Hey now, love. Out for a pull?" She asked - looking the young woman up and down, "I prefer a good *dobber*, but I'm up for it. (*Hiccup*) You are a buff, *aintcha*?"

The cloaked woman stopped in front of Polly and removed her hood. Her voice was soft - but remained as expressionless as her face, "I am looking for Kiya?"

Polly raised her eyebrows while closing one eye in an attempt to maintain some rational thought, "I'm game love, what is a *Kiya*?"

"I had heard that she lives near you. Perhaps in your Doss house. She carries the Cratalis in her womb. Do you know her?"

Polly staggered a bit. "I know a Kelly, but no Kiya," she slurred - trying to smile. "But If it's a *cradling* be your thing, four pence will get your end away."

Polly steadied herself against a nearby door that opened into a stable yard. It swung open unexpectedly, causing her to lose her balance. The pretty young lady was suddenly upon her, pushing her through the open stable door - knocking her to the ground. Fast as lightening, the young woman flashed her hand across Polly's face.

At first, Polly was unsure as to what had occurred. *"Don't be so beastly,"* she tried to say. But nothing came from her mouth but a low gurgle. Baffled and horrified at what was occurring, she watched as the pretty young lady turned her smiling face toward a strange red spray that seemed to come from nowhere. Her throat felt strange and she began to feel a bizarre tugging at her stomach. Everything seemed to become surreal as a bitter cold enveloped her. Weariness gave Polly the thought that she would close her eyes for just a second, but she died before managing even that simple task. The last thing she saw was the pretty young lady wrist deep inside of her abdomen.

Searching.

London England - Whitechapel; November 9th, 1888

The church clock could be heard striking two am and George Hutchinson turned his collar toward the chill, damp fog that had settled over London. It had finally stopped raining but as most residents of London knew, the reprieve was likely to be short lived.

Hutchinson - or simply *Hutch* as most of the residents of Whitechapel called him - didn't care much for the mid-autumn weather of London. The cold and wet just reminded him that winter was coming and summer was still a good deal off.

He readjusted his tattered muffler and concentrated as best he could on the wet, cobblestone sidewalk. He had emptied his pockets at the

Princess Alice pub house and was now a bit regretful that - in doing so - he may have forfeited his bed at the *Victoria Lodgings*.

He stumbled along down Commercial Street towards the *Willmott's* doss house on Flowers and Dean Street. He had a friend that had a bunk he could possibly share and if not, the nearby Queens Head Pub offered a decent chance of scoring a pint with a game of darts. He was in the mood for drink anyways and he supposed at this point - win or lose - his bed could wait.

He was doing a fairly good job at keeping one foot in front of the other. At least he thought he was. The cheap Irish swill he'd been drinking all night was wreaking havoc with his focus.

'Goddamn Irish,' he thought.

As he approached Thrawl Street, he staggered just a bit - overcorrected turning his ankle over a stone and lurched blindly the opposite way. There was no correction this time and he stumbled straight into the unyielding body of a stranger that was standing on the corner.

Where had he come from?

The stranger had not been there just a second ago. At least Hutch didn't think he had. But in his admittedly inebriated condition, he couldn't be sure.

"My apologies, mate. I be humbled for my behavior," Hutch slurred - spying the fancy spats on the man's boots and the stylish Great Coat with matching felt Bowler hat.

'A proper geezer for being in the Rookery,' Hutch thought. "Even more humbled in asking for kindness," he begged - holding out his hat. "Sir?"

"Stop drinking, perhaps you might have a penny," The dapper gentleman replied - offering nothing else to Hutchinson but an ominous stare.

So intense was the man's stare that Hutch suddenly couldn't breathe. The man's coal black eyes bore through him with an unspeakable intensity. It was as if the stranger possessed a terrifying, timeless energy. The man reached out and grabbed Hutch's arm and when he did, it were as if time stopped. Silence enveloped the city; the sounds of the night abruptly terminating. As if time had inhaled sharply and forgot to exhale. It was an eerie, out of place experience and Hutch's head swam in delirium. Dazed, he stumbled backwards and away from the stranger's grip.

The stranger appeared to shimmer in the glow of the dim street-corner lamp. Hutch closed his eyes and rubbed them with the back of his hand figuring he must be more intoxicated than he thought. Putting his hat back on his head, he stumbled across the intersection - continuing his journey up Commercial Street towards Flowers and Dean Street.

Recovering from his bizarre encounter, Hutch saw someone walking toward him. His heart skipped, causing him to block the disturbing memory of the strange man for a short time. He recognized the person as the sweet angel of Miller's Court; Miss Mary. The pretty lass that lived just up Dorset Street. She was always kind with word and after employing her services a time or two, he had to admit that he had fallen for the young lady.

Although he also had to confess that his love remained unrequited.

"Mary!" Hutchinson smiled - hoping to engage the pretty lady in conversation.

"*'Allo*, Hutch. How you fairing this cold night," Mary replied - brushing a dripping strand of hair from her eyes and dabbing her wet fingers on her apron.

"It could always be better, although I did take a visit at the Romford market yesterday," Hutch said proudly - hoping to impress.

"*Romford*?" Mary exclaimed - raising an eyebrow. "My, aren't you a dandy? Perhaps a *tanner* that I can warm my own bones, then?"

Hutch's smile faded. "Sorry Mary, I'm in a bit of a *zwodder* and I don't even have a ha' penny - much less four pence for my own bed," Hutchinson replied - dejected and now embarrassed that he could not help his damsel in distress.

"Tough luck love, I need to carry my own lodge." Mary smiled - spying the stranger that Hutchison had run into at the corner. "Appears a posh punter, what? I'm off then." She breathed a soft sigh - offering a light peck to George Hutchinson's cheek.

"We could pool ourselves and you don't have to do such awful work," Hutch called after her - desperately trying to engage her just a bit more.

Mary laughed, "Perhaps, but not tonight, love. You said yourself, you don't even have a ha' penny to your name."

Hutch eyed the stranger down the block that had suddenly appeared in front of him. The man was walking their way - slowly. Whistling a tune. The memory of their encounter - just a few minutes earlier - gave Hutch the shivers. "Careful, Mary."

Mary looked over her shoulder at Hutch and sighed, "I have to make a living, Hutch. You know that Joseph has left me."

"I know, just be careful," he said again. "That Whitechapel ripper still be about."

Mary Kelly laughed, ignoring the pleadings of George Hutchinson and staggered in pursuit of the approaching stranger. Her voice echoing across the buildings as she sang, "♪*Scenes of my childhood arise before my gaze, Bringing recollections of bygone happy days...*♪"

Hutch watched in silence as Mary Kelly came upon the stranger with a giggle, her singing falling ominously silent. She said something to the stranger he couldn't hear but it seemed to him that Mary knew the man.

How would she know him? He wondered.

The two of them stood at the corner for a small time - talking - the man touching Mary's shoulder. Hutch could feel the jealousy boiling inside him. He decided to forgo Willmott's flop house and instead, began his trek another block - towards the Queen's Head Pub. He could hear Mary and the stranger behind him - still talking.

He stopped at the corner of Fashion Street and leaned against a light pole in front of the Queen's Head Pub - pretending to tie his shoe. He watched as Mary and the stranger continued on past. Mary not even looking up at him.

Hutch's heart fell just a bit at her unintentional rebuke.

Mary's left arm was intertwined with the stranger's right. The strange man held a small, wrapped item in his left hand - Hutch noticed. He immediately turned his gaze when the stranger looked at him, unwilling to endure that unnatural stare again - the man was unnerving.

"You'll be all right," Hutch heard the stranger say.

"All right," Kelly replied.

The pit in his stomach churned as Hutch watched them walk towards the Dorset street corner. Hutch had come to grips with what Mary did for a living, but this stranger was something different. With the Whitechapel Ripper - the press had taken to calling *Jack* - running around. George Hutchinson was suddenly very apprehensive. The Whitechapel Ripper had already disemboweled three other women - all of them prostitutes. And he simply didn't trust this fancy bloke that had so enamored Mary. Everything about the man was creepy.

It had started to rain again as Hutch crossed the street in pursuit of the two, observing them from a distance as they turned into the entrance of Miller's court. Hurrying after them, he watched as Mary tried to open the door to her little room inside the court. She wore no hat and had to swipe continuously at the rainwater running into her face.

"I lost my kerchief," Mary Kelly said.

George Hutchinson's breath caught as he watched the stranger reach into his jacket pocket. He sighed in relief when the man merely produced a red handkerchief and offered it to Mary. Mary wiped the water from her face and kissed the stranger on the cheek. "Thank you, Love," she said.

Opening the door to her little room, Mary Kelly led the strange man inside - closing the door behind them.

13 Miller's Court, Whitechapel, London; November 9th, 1888. 4:00 am

"How did you find me?" Mary asked.

Not yet answering, the man peered around the austere room - his eyes coming to rest on a painting above the mantle. He stared for a long moment at it. The canvas depicted a distraught young woman being consoled by an older woman. The anguish of the young woman - burying her torment in the lap of an older woman - spoke to him. The detail of the art was exquisite - a remarkable emotional depiction - and he decided to add the original to his collection. He made a mental note to discover the original work's location.

Noticing the man's interest in the picture - Mary Kelly explained, "It's called '*The Fisherman's Widow*'. It reminds me that all things end and the sorrow of lost love."

The man nodded - absently. His attention now diverted to the room's other entrapments. He raked his gloved finger across the fireplace mantel - turning his lip in disgust. Mary decided not to comment.

He turned from the fireplace with a sniff, "I have been following my brother from America into Europe," the man said. "He has the Orb with him. I left America some weeks ago in his pursuit and have taken a small house in London while attempting to regain his trail. When Cithimay informed me that you may be here, I tasked her to search for you."

Mary lowered her eyes to the floor and sighed. She removed her wet dress and petticoat and hung it near the fireplace mantel to dry. "I haven't felt the touch of the Orb since I have been here, or I would have surely left." - She shook her head - "Our brother - Ah-Vel - has not kept his promise."

The man touched Mary's shoulder - giving it a gentle squeeze. "Tonight your prayers shall be answered; we will leave this dreadful place. But we need to get you to safety, now that our daughter is coming close to finding you."

Mary nodded heavily, "Cithimay has already been round to see me."

The man raised his eyes, his expression otherwise unreadable.

"She calls herself Lizzie right now." Mary frowned in thought, "She seemed a touch peculiar. She made me uneasy and I was grateful when Joseph arrived for a visit."

"She is looking for the Cratalis," the man explained.

Mary's laugh was abrupt, "*Hah*!" Standing up, she checked the drying progress of her dress. "I do not know where the Cratalis is and wouldn't care anyway. Ah-Vel sent me to this dreadful island when Alysia fell. Hoping I should disappear." Mary turned to look at the man, "Hoping I would escape from you." She returned to folding her nearly dry apron, "But this place is hell. There is nothing you or our daughter can do to me that this place hasn't already taken."

She suddenly turned to the man with a realization, "The Whitechapel Ripper; it was Cithimay looking for me, wasn't it?"

The man nodded solemnly - walking to the hearth and using a poker to stoke the flames.

Mary was shocked - tears beginning to well, "I don't understand. Why is she cutting those women up?"

The man took a deep breath - slowly releasing it, "She is following a rumor."

Mary was aghast - turning, "*A bloody rumor?*"

"A rumor has passed down through the years concerning a passage written in Ta-Huti's manuscript. It would indicate that the last of the Cratalis was placed within the womb of an Alysian Elder. She concluded that you might be that missing courtier."

"*A bloody rumor!*" Mary repeated.

Silence settled - heavy - then, "She is my daughter, but yet she is a stranger." Mary began to cry.

Eventually, she wiped her eyes and asked, "How is my son? How is Ta-Vil?"

The man settled the poker in its holder, "He is why I am here, Kiya. I need to resurrect him, but I cannot keep them both leashed to me. And I cannot endure a second *Sacrament of the Symbi*. I am already tethered to

Cithimay." - The man sighed with weariness - "I sent Cithimay to find you, but her desire for the Cratalis is overshadowing any good judgment. I needed to find you before she did." - The man lifted his chin with calm decisiveness - "I will take you back to my retreat. You will be safe there. While I quench our daughter's impetuousness."

"*No.*"

The man frowned, puzzled.

"You ask for more heartache, Ka-Yin. If there are any children that *Ah-Tum* ever cursed a parent with, it be those two. I would rather they fall to nature than offer myself to their perpetual existence. No, I will not be a part of this."

"I cannot do this alone. They are our children," the man pleaded.

"I will not, Ka-Yin. There is a reason Ah-Vel chose to hide me from you. In all this time, I had all but forgotten. But you coming here reminds me. They are dark seeds. Both of them should be purged from this earth. You should do well as to relieve yourself of their burden, Ka-Yin. Do not ask me to undertake their existence. To endure that which you have given. For I cannot."

The man looked at her for a long moment. His face unreadable. Finally, he breathed a heavy sigh - his eyelids closed in sorrow. "You forget Kiya. I only need your heart."

Mary stared in shocked disbelief, "I don't understand."

"I believe you do," Ka-Yin said calmly. "I am bound to a mission to retrieve the Orb from my brother. I prefer to have all of you by my side. But with your refusal, please be reminded that our daughter may have the rest of you - as long as I have your heart."

Without warning, a cloaked figure suddenly shimmered into existence inside the little room.

"Ka-Yin, No! *You wouldn't!*"

"Oh, but in a heartbeat - my dear." Ka-Yin tilted his head - a smile forming, "Or more specifically, *your* heartbeat."

The heavy cloak suddenly dropped to the floor to reveal the naked figure of a beautiful woman. Her face downcast as her ambivalent eyes - brilliant green - gazed upwards to Kiya. For a moment she remained stock still. A long, sharp dagger held to her side.

Kiya's dress now dry, Ka-Yin removed it from the mantle and began to neatly fold the garment. He placed the dry clothing on a nearby table. "We are not monsters," he said. "But you must admit Kiya, we are duty bound. And all I need is your heart to resurrect our son."

With lightening speed, Cithimay descended upon her mother and began slicing her body past the point of any modicum of decency.

"*Murder!*" Mary managed to shriek. But within an instant, her throat had been sliced - silencing any further screaming.

Revealing her womb, Cithimay quickly searched and unsheathed the organ. As an immortal elder, Kiya still clung to life for several lingering, hell-darkened moments until her heart was mercifully sliced from her chest.

Ka-Yin retrieved Kiya's still beating heart from his daughters grasp along with a small section of her thymus gland before shimmering into the night, leaving his daughter to her unholy mission.

Shimmering into his retreat - deep inside the Colorado Rocky Mountains - Schulte placed Kiya's emancipated heart in a special jar - immersed within a harvested liquid of her body's own Cratalis fluid. He then placed the jar on a shelf in his private chamber, watching absently as it continued to beat against the glass.

"Dain," he said quietly.

The giant dark man instantly glimmered into existence behind him.

"Please give my daughter some help, if you don't mind."

As Dain shimmered into a time stream, Schulte tenderly cared for his new prize. "You shall be our son's guiding light, my love."

Gently he touched the jar, feeling how the muscle thudded against the glass.

"*My Kiya,*" he whispered.

About The Author

W.C. resides in Colorado with his family. He is a proud father, grandfather and a devoted husband. He is a musician and woodworker and enjoys spending his time creating new things.

As a child, his family would take trips around the United States visiting historical sites from Gettysburg to Dealey plaza and from Atlanta to Deadwood. These visits would be underscored with an emphasis on their historical significance.

As a pre-teen, his father would entertain him with fictionalized stories of the places they had visited based around the actual history.

"His stories were wildly entertaining and I remember them quite fondly, but more so they became an enticement to study history with relish and ignited the desire to create my own fiction centered on mankind's most significant historical moments."

The Lownsbury Chronicles is W.C. Wallbaum's opus of that effort centered on (Among various infamous events) one of the greatest stories ever told that resonates to this day. Many of the characters in *"The Lownsbury Chronicles; The Machine"* are based upon actual people and actual events. It is encouraged that the reader performs their own research on the characters to learn about them and pull even greater appreciation of the recorded historical events that unfolded.

"I have, of course, taken liberties based on numerous theological theories and actual scripture, but have nonetheless held true to my own passionate theories of past events in many cases; often taking current events as a guide to past occurrences."

The first book - "First Strike" - introduces us to our cast of characters and offers mysterious insight to the part each will play. The second book - "Second Options" - brings us a little deeper into the mystery to have a complete understanding of our story within the third book - "Third Rule" - where all is revealed.

No matter your own beliefs, it is a sincere hope you enjoy and are enticed to research more into the beliefs that have led the world since their inception.

"As my father would always teach - Everyone should have a solid understanding of what it is they believe and, more importantly, why they believe it"

189

W.C. Wallbaum

www.ingramcontent.com/pod-product-compliance
Lightning Source LLC
Chambersburg PA
CBHW022149240626
47153CB00007B/2586